Coldhearted & Crazy:

Say U Promise 1

Coldhearted & Crazy:

Say U Promise 1

Ms. Michel Moore

www.urbanbooks.net

Urban Books, LLC
97 N18th Street
Wyandanch, NY 11798

ISBN 13: 978-1-60162-613-4
ISBN 10: 1-60162-613-4

First Trade Paperback Printing July 2014
Printed in the United States of America

10 9 8 7 6 5 4 3 2

Distributed by Kensington Publishing Corp.
Submit Wholesale Orders to:
Kensington Publishing Corp.
C/O Penguin Group (USA) Inc.
Attention: Order Processing
405 Murray Hill Parkway
East Rutherford, NJ 07073-2316
Phone: 1-800-526-0275
Fax: 1-800-227-9604

Coldhearted & Crazy:

Say U Promise 1

by

Ms. Michel Moore

The Jump Off

How did this happen? How did I get here? Here to this point. These little simple-minded third-generation punks done got the drop on me! Well, I'll be damned, three damn young kids. I swear on everything I love, I can still smell the breast milk on their stankin' foul, immature breaths. Yet, here I lie stretched out in my best suit ready for a Saturday night of partying. I'm covered with dirt. My pants leg torn at the knee and my snakeskin shoes scuffed the hell up. These murdering sons of bitches! They straight caught me slippin'. Why did I come tonight? Why?

In between my coldhearted stares of these pint-sized killers, I see the small dark pools of blood slowly growing from Melinda's gunshot wounds: one in her side, one near her collarbone. My loyal queen was gasping for air as she choked on her own mucus. I grew infuriated seeing her suffer like she was. I had a love so strong for her as well as the love we shared; our bond was unbreakable. Melinda was more than just my wife. She was the mother of my two precious daughters, my best friend, and my road dawg. Me-Me, as I'd always called her, was damn near my everything and because of my arrogant, stubborn ways, the woman who'd birthed my seeds now lies inches away from me, dying, and I can't do anything to help her. How really messed up is that?

I mean I really dropped the damn ball this go-around. Make no mistake, this one's all on me.

Why didn't I just wait for my brother like Melinda begged me to do? I really didn't trust these young cats off rip, but as usual I thought I was bigger than the game and the rules didn't apply to me. Stupid me. I'd violated every rule of the game and was now paying the ultimate price. I'd just met these busters looking for a quick come up and was letting them cop from me on the humble. What can I say? My bad! I got greedy and wanted that money. Shit, I ain't gonna lie. It started gettin' good to a guy. Me and mines was eating good, driving good, dressing good, smoking good, and riding good. We were what poor folk around our way considered hood rich and we played our part well.

They say loot will change a person; hell, I can testify to that shit. Flat out, it got me off my square. I fucked up this time. No doubt! How could I believe in any honor among thieves? It didn't exist. How could I have forgotten the basic levels of being in the life? The rules of the dope game never ever change, just the players. Live by the gun, blah, blah, blah, shit's tight now. Time is ticking. I'm not brand new to the streets. I've been around death long enough to realize that my wifey, Melinda, has just taken her last breath in this lifetime and I, as hard as I was fighting it, was undoubtedly next in line for that same fate.

I'll be damned, here it comes. I can't feel my left lower leg anymore. Now the right! The last bullet these assholes let loose caused a burning sensation that ripped right through my flesh, knocking me off my feet and in this ditch. Still wishing for a different outcome, I wanted to beg for them to spare my wife's life, but I had no intention of going out like a straight bitch. I have my pride, and if nothing else but on point and principle, I'm gonna keep it gangsta 'til the very end. Besides, I knew my Me-Me was already gone. The mother of my two daughters was dead, finished, over, and it was my damn fault. Yeah, it's pretty much a wrap, for both her and me.

If I could turn back the hands of time, I still wouldn't change a motherfucking thang. I can't say I honestly regret one minute of it. Me and my girl had a ball doing what we did, living how we lived. Just thinking about slangin' could get my manhood rock hard. From being posted on the corner of Linwood Avenue, taking two dollar shorts on a top side hit of powder to grinding up on my first cake of that good stuff, that shit was real, hell sometimes maybe even too real. My sweetheart, Melinda, was with me from day one. She always had my back. Now here we go again, but this time we won't be able to get high and laugh this one off.

I feel myself getting weaker as the seconds drag by. It's about that time. The clock is about to stop. I know I've done wrong and more than likely the devil has left the light on for me. That's okay though. I earned my spot in hell. But God, if you can still hear me, for Melinda's sake, please take care of our little daughters, Kenya and London; especially Kenya, who has an inner rage and a lust for the streets just like her old man. They're the purest thing that came out of all this madness. Game over, lights out!

From da cradle to the fuckin' grave!

Chapter One

Two of a Kind

Buzzzzzzzzzzz . . . It was a typical morning in the small family household located in the middle of the crime-infested Detroit neighborhood. The digital alarm clock was making what seemed like an intolerable sound, yet there was still no movement from either one of the "different as night and day" teenage twins. The alarm going off on the clock at 6:45 a.m. every school day was a normal occurrence, just as normal as the girls trying to ignore the sound and their grandmother's sometimes annoying voice.

"Get up!" Gran, cane in hand, yelled with a Southern drawl even though she'd been living up North in the city for decades. "Both of you gals get up before you're late!" Every morning was the same routine. She thought, *Lord have mercy, don't let these girls end up like their mother Melinda because if they do, I don't know what in the world I will do!*

Gran had two children of her own. Melinda was her youngest, her baby. Everyone knew she'd tried her very best with both of her loving children, but to no avail; the black-hearted streets had other plans for them. Both had died young living the life she wanted so desperately for them to leave alone. Her son, just barely eighteen, had overdosed on drugs, heroin to be exact; and Melinda, who always thought she was too smart for her own good, was found shot to death in the projects in a ditch with her husband, leaving the girls, her only children, orphans.

Hattie Jean Lewis was a devout Christian woman, who stood tall in her faith and love for the Lord. She used to stay up countless nights and shed many a tear, worrying about her little girl. *Damn, why did she have to meet that low-down, good-for-nothing Johnnie Roberts?* Gran frowned up her face questioning why things had gone so wrong. *Sorry, Lord.* She quickly repeated over and over, *Let thy will be done. If you thought it was best to call them home, I know you know best and only you can help me with these girls, especially Kenya.*

Gran started loudly singing church hymns; that always got the entire household up and going. Not because the twins love hearing them, but the complete opposite. Whenever it came to going to church one of the sisters, Kenya of course, always bucked at the idea. She was considered the wild child of the two and everyone who would encounter the girls could easily tell the difference. Gran didn't care how much Kenya rebelled. God was the head of her household and Kenya, London, and anyone else who stepped foot inside her home was going to follow suit. Gran would drag Kenya to services week after week praying she would soften her heart. From experience, the old woman knew good and well that everyone would need and call upon the Lord one day, Kenya included.

With a "mad at the world" attitude, Amoya Kenya Roberts was the first one of the girls to jump out the bed. The second verse of her grandmother's song was unbearable to the young teen.

"Morning, baby." Gran tried to kiss her on her forehead, but Ms. Kenya, waving her hand backward, was having none of that. Since the twins' first names were so close, everyone called them by their middle names.

Kenya was what you would call the most outgoing one of the two. She often joked and kept a smile on her face; that was, as long as she was having her own way, which she often demanded. Having a thirst for being the center of attention, she was most certainly the life of the party. However, just as easy as the jokes, smiles, and laughter could begin, they could be brought to a screeching halt. Kenya possessed a short-fuse firecracker temper that was unbelievable. The teen with a beautiful face, loved by some and hated by others, could and would snap just like that at a drop of a hat. Kenya was truly her father's daughter in every way you could imagine, from personality and demeanor to his hustle by any means to get paid pedigree. And for that reason, among many more, her immediate family worried about her and what unseen tragedies that mentality could ultimately bring to her.

Amia London Roberts was the latter of the girls to get up and start her day. "Hey, Gran." She smiled as she reached out to her granny. Knowing another day wasn't promised to anyone, she hugged and kissed her every chance that she got.

"Mornin', baby. I love you."

"I love you too, Gran." London beamed with joy as her sister came out the bathroom, interrupting their embrace.

"Dang, why y'all two gotta be so mushy all the time? It's too early in the morning!" Kenya asked while turning her lip up, "And, London, why don't you stop being such a butt kisser? I mean dang!"

London paid her sister no mind. She loved her grandmother. They would discus all sorts of important subjects. Prejudice and racism in America and civil rights struggles that had taken place in Alabama and throughout the South. They shared conversations about Dr. King, Malcolm X, and even the Black Panthers organization. Not only did London like to hear about the struggle of her people, she promised

Gran one day to be part of the solution. The honor-roll teen loved to read books and would spend countless hours at the library. She would study every chance she got, even at night when the troubled neighborhood she lived in was quiet and still or her sister was chattering away on the phone.

While London spent her nights studying, Kenya would stay posted on the phone. She could often hold a conversation for what seemed like hours on end talking about absolutely nothing of any value. Meeting different boys at the mall and exchanging phone numbers, she'd tell them all kind of things a normal fourteen-year-old had no business knowing about life in general, let alone repeating. Everywhere she'd go, the boys, some her own age and some much older, flocked around Kenya like bees to honey, but London didn't care one bit. Her only focus was obtaining and maintaining good grades and a high GPA. Their Gran had taught London that knowledge was true power, and with a good education, she could easily write her own ticket in life.

London always daydreamed, wondering if her mother had stayed in school and hit the books as much as she heard that she'd hit the streets getting into mischief with her dad, would she still be alive today. Nevertheless, bottom line, Kenya, not giving a damn about jack shit, was hell-bent on living her young life recklessly and London, determined to make something of hers, studied, wanting to be labeled something other than a hood rat.

Both London and Kenya got dressed for school. They were only fourteen, but each had already developed their own style of dress. Kenya picked out a pair of light blue jeans that were neatly pressed and had a jacket and baby T-shirt to match. She grabbed her new designer bag and belt, throwing them on the bed. After finally pouring herself into her pants, she turned around in the mirror and smiled as she thought, *Both tight and right.*

"Humph, should I were my K-Swiss or my new Air Force 1s?" she then questioned out loud, still checking out her own ass.

"I think you should wear the K-Swiss," London whispered under her breath.

"Did you say something over there Miss Power to the People?" Kenya had a smirk across her face, turning to face London. Kenya loved her sister, true enough, but she knew the girl had no taste whatsoever. "K-Swiss you said, then I know it's the Forces today." They both shared a laugh as London playfully threw her pillow across the room at her twin.

London pulled out a pair of black slacks and a plain black polo shirt. She wasn't into all of those high-priced designer clothes that her sister liked. Why walk around with someone else's name plastered across your chest and behind? Why be a free walking billboard on display? *Free promotion and advertisement for the white man, I don't think so. No way, not the kid,* she thought as she watched Kenya get dressed.

They both had long sandy-brown hair that stretched past their shoulders. Kenya always let hers hang and flow wildly, while London favored hers pulled back off the face in a ponytail. Their features were identical. If not for their clothes and obvious different characteristics, many of their own distant family members and friends couldn't tell the twins apart. With two different agendas for the day, they were out the door on their way to school—separately.

Chapter Two

Kenya

"I hope none of these fake thirsty snakes try to start no bullshit with me today. I'm definitely not in the fucking mood for their messy asses!" Just as Kenya turned the end of the long block she spotted Carmen. She was her girl, for real, for real; her best friend. If ever there was a female who had your back no matter what happened or jumped off, it would be her. Kenya had been in serious physical altercations with groups of jealous girls several times over, and Carmen was always there standing right beside Kenya, if not in front of her, showing their opponents what was really good with them both.

Carmen smirked, tugging down on her skirt. "What up, twin? What's happening?" Carmen always smiled when she said that shit because she knew that it irked Kenya. Her friend always wanted to be known for her own identity. As far as Kenya was concerned London was London and she was herself, twin or not.

"Very funny. Ha-ha, motherfucker, very funny. I been told your ass about that twin shit! I didn't know I had my own personal comedian to walk to school with!" Kenya snapped.

"Damn, girl, is that a new hookup you rocking? That shit is seriously hot to death. I know that ain't no regular off-the-rack shit, is it? You've been straight holding out on this one!"

Kenya was cheesin' from ear to ear, taking in every last one of the compliments Carmen was dishing out. Kenya knew there wasn't a girl from miles around who could fade her style or unique way of rocking her gear. Everywhere she went, people would be on her envious of her wardrobe.

The girls' uncle was always showering them with money, jewelry, and, most importantly of all to a stuck-up Kenya, clothes. The majority of their gear he would get from New York or Cali. Sometimes he'd even have his weave shop owner girlfriend pick out and send garments back from overseas when she'd travel. After his older brother, Johnnie, and his sister-in-law got murdered back in the day, he always tried to look out for his little nieces the best he could. Even when he'd get locked up, which was quite often considering the ruthless lifestyle he lived, he made sure he had his woman continue to hold the twins down. Gran, knowing it was blood money he was spending, didn't like all the expensive gifts he gave the girls, but what could she do? He was their family also: blood. Matter of fact, he was the only one out of the Roberts family who even tried to maintain a relationship with both London and Kenya after their mom died. She knew he truly loved his nieces and would die for them if need be and Gran respected that fact.

Finally, after letting Carmen go on and on with her praise, Kenya, extremely loyal to her friends, told her she would gladly let her have some of the pieces that she didn't want or couldn't fit in.

"Thanks, girl, I love you." Carmen started trying to hug her friend for always looking out even though she didn't have to.

"Urgg fall back, chick! What I tell your ass 'bout all that kissy-lovey shit? Save that for them busters you be dealing with," Kenya hissed, trying to play that hard role.

Carmen looked at her girl and shook her head. If ever there was a person in need of a hug and some affection it was Kenya. Carmen knew that her best friend had major issues with trusting or loving anyone or anything. She didn't know or even care to know where Kenya had developed those feelings, because everyone in their Detroit hood had their own problems and demons to deal with and she and Kenya were no different. Life was hard in the Motor City.

As they slow strolled down Linwood Avenue, the pair encountered all types of ghetto hood antics, from early morning junkies bold looking to get a fix, to bums fighting in the middle of the street over the last sip of a warm beer some stranger had just tossed out the window. The classmates could have just as well taken the side streets and avoided all the turmoil of street life, but the girls loved to fuck with the "common folk" as they called them: "Y'all girls look pretty today, can you spare a dollar? Get an education, do you have a quarter?" or "I'm trying to get something to eat and I need thirty-five cents."

Kenya, immune to sympathy for the next person's bad luck in life, had heard every crackhead, drug addict, and sorry-ass story in the book known to man. Sometimes she and Carmen wouldn't hesitate humoring themselves by making them do outlandish things no sane human being would even consider. She would have them bark like a dog for fifty cents or imitate other farm animals for their own childish amusement. There was no limit to what they could easily encourage a Detroit crackhead to do if the price was right. And since times were so hard and cold in the city, the price was always right.

As Kenya and Carmen passed the liquor store, Daisy appeared. She was a middle-aged woman hard in the face strung out on heroin, who used to be friends with both Kenya's parents and wouldn't let the young teen forget it.

No matter where the girls would go in the economically stressed neighborhood of longtime homeowners, they were reminded about their deceased parents' impact on the community and its residents, whether they were fond memories or not.

"Yeah, me, your mama, and daddy used to get our souls proper back in the day! All top side, uncut! That good shit!" Daisy rocked from side to side to the imaginary music that was playing in her drug-infested mind. "I'm telling you, Kenya or London or whichever one you is, your daddy only copped the best shit this damn city ever seen! Oh yeah! Ol' Johnnie Roberts knew how to play the game, for real!"

Always begging for this, that, and the third, she felt Kenya and London were obligated to give her spare change whenever she asked for it just on the strength that she and their parents shared needles or blow from time to time. Some mornings, this one in particular, Kenya was in one of her moods and cruelly decided to make Daisy dance for a dollar, recording it on her cell phone so she could laugh at it later and post on Facebook. After humiliating her parents' less fortunate friend with not much coaxing, she and Carmen ran off giggling.

"What's so funny, y'all?" It was Allan, their homeboy from around the way. Randomly, he always seemed to appear out of nowhere when they least expected him to. He always walked with the girls to school. "I said what's so damn funny? Why y'all laughing so hard?" He gave both of his friends a stupid look as he repeated his question, not receiving an answer the first time. They girls looked at each other and busted out laughing again.

"Nothing, nothing." Kenya was wiping the tears off her face. "It's just I didn't know that people could be so desperate that's all."

Allan never got the joke and the girls let it go, especially because Allan's mom was a closet head. Ain't no true secrets in the hood and his mother's smoking crack most certainly wasn't one of them. Everything in the dark always comes to light, please believe. Sure she didn't hang on the corner selling pussy or begging for bottles like Daisy's good dancing ass or the other no-pride-having addicts, but a head was a head, bottom line. It wasn't any true shame to what your kinfolk did. Like Daisy always pointed out, way back it was cool to snort a line or shoot a li'l somethin'-somethin' into your veins, but now a dopefiend was treated like public enemy number one. But in the here and now, as long as it wasn't you yourself getting high sucking the glass dick, it was all good. Hell, everyone had a fool somewhere in their family tree. That was life.

The trio finally arrived at Central High School. While Allan was a junior for the second time, both of the girls were only freshman, but you damn straight couldn't tell by the reception they received. As soon as they cleared the metal detector, it was all smiles and handshakes on their end for the most part. Every guy in the school wanted to get with Kenya if they weren't gay, and of course her ever-present sidekick Carmen came along for the ride. Even the upperclassmen, who usually didn't fuck with crab-ass freshmen, would stop what they were doing to gawk at the girls' asses bounce by in those tight jeans or hooker short skirts that the two were infamous for wearing. But of course as always there had to be haters on deck lurking. You know that bullshit goes without saying. Hell, real talk, haters make the world go round and what school wasn't blessed with them, Central students included, who regularly took hatin' on the next person, in particular her, to the next level on a day-to-day basis.

"They should rename this bitch Hater High but that might be too much like right!" Kenya blurted out loud as she mean mugged a few chicks who were giving her just as much shade and fever as she was giving them.

As much attention as the fellas gave Kenya and Carmen, the other girls would stare them down and often roll their eyes at the pair. Truthfully speaking, there was not one single female who really liked the conceited pair. However, Kenya made it perfectly clear she couldn't care less if any bitch in the entire school liked her or not; they were damn sure gonna respect her. She was settling for nothing less.

"Hey, ladies, I like your outfits." One girl grinned at Carmen and Kenya, while trying to be a real smart-ass.

Kenya peeped that shit out and let the girl have it Kenya Roberts style. "Girl, I like your outfit too. I know I say that every week when you wear it, but it's so cute." Carmen and Kenya gave each other the side eye and snickered as they left the dusty female looking and feeling stupid as hell for even trying it in the first place.

"You crazy!" Carmen was smiling and falling against the locker after Kenya had cleverly checked one of their many frenemies.

"Man, fuck that skank-a-dank low-budget bird! She runs around here, always trying to be slick-mouthed all the time like her own shit don't stank. Imagine that whore trying to come for me!" Kenya huffed, caught up in her emotions. "She should try putting that jaw of hers to better use and maybe, just maybe, one of those losers she fucks with would upgrade that yesteryear wardrobe she be rocking!" Kenya tried to hold her laughter as she gave the girl one more casually fake smile from across the hall as she entered her class. Once she made it inside the classroom and took her seat, Kenya was quickly surrounded by guys wanting a few minutes of her time.

After a few moments of her holding court, the bell rang for the start of first period.

London

"I love you, Gran!" London lovingly told her with affection as she left out the front door. *Let me double check. I've got all my books, my homework and my lunch.* London always took her own lunch so she could sit under a tree and study if she found time. As she slowly walked down her block, the compassionate teen always took time to speak to all of her neighbors, asking if each was having a good day. She, unlike her sister, was friendly to everyone, which was why everyone on the entire close-knit block loved London much more than her cynical-minded twin.

At the very end of the street barely stood the house where Amber and her family lived. She was London's best friend ever since she was four years old and came to live with Gran. Even though she had her sister to play with, Amber made living on Glendale bearable. At first London seemed to miss her old toddler playmates, her own bed, and her own house, not to mention both her parents, but with the love of Gran and the friendship of Amber, she would grow into her new life without any noticeable problems.

"Hey, girl."

"Hey, Amber." London returned her friend's smile.

"Did you get a chance to finish that report in English you were working on?" Amber had a sympathetic look on her face, hoping for the best. She knew all the hell that her best friend London caught trying to study at home; with Kenya blasting the radio half the night and talking on the phone the other half, London fought hard to keep her grades up and her sanity intact.

"Yeah, I got it finished, finally. The teacher wanted at most four pages, but I ended up with six and a half. I tried to cut some down," London said nonchalantly, always known for overdoing it when it came to schoolwork.

Amber grinned, telling London the exact same thing she said after every A paper that London received. "Please don't forget the little people when you become president one day." They both smiled as they continued walking down the same side street they took every day.

"Hello, girls." The old lady who walked her little dog every morning waved.

"Hi," they answered in unison.

They always stopped to talk to old Mr. Phelps. He was practically blind and a lot of kids in the neighborhood would throw stuff on his porch to scare him and always left his gate wide open. He being eighty-one and blind made him an easy target for kids and drug addicts alike who often took advantage of his disabilities. London, known for being overly nice, would sometimes lose her temper, like her sister, and get in the zone falling into the dark side. It didn't happen often, but seeing some of her peers mess with the elderly or people who couldn't stand up and defend themselves was one surefire way to get London up in arms and to prove she was also her father's daughter.

"Hey, Mr. Phelps," the girls yelled up to the porch where he sat every morning. "How you doing? Do you need anything on our way back from school?" they both inquired.

"No, girls, I'm fine, just fine. I'm just getting some of that good morning air, thanks for asking." Mr. Phelps smiled and thought how nice London and Amber both were. He knew those two girls were going to be somebody someday. Especially London, who'd always made sure on Sundays to bring him by a healthy plate that her Gran would cook.

"I hope there's not going to be a science test today," London stated while kicking a can down the street.

"Me too," Amber agreed as the high school came in sight.

Both girls chatted between themselves about school, homework, and other things that teenage girls talked about: boys. Although her sister was the self-proclaimed diva of Detroit's Central High, London went through school practically unnoticed by both boys and girls alike. The only people at school who noticed Amia London Roberts were her teachers. She was the only one in class who would turn in all of her assignments on time, sometimes the only one who turned them in period. They admired her ambition. Yet, some of the least enthusiastic instructors hated the fact that London had a lot more knowledge than they possessed on most subjects and never once seemed to let them forget that fact.

Some teachers just wanted to cash their paychecks, avoid conflict, and go home to their families. However, London was having none of that. She had a thirst for knowledge and made all her teachers earn their salary, each and every penny. Gran used to joke that London had been here before, and many she'd encounter believed her grandmother's assessment to be true.

As London and Amber entered through the doors of school, they went their separate ways. London went in and out the crowds with ease. She didn't want to bump into anyone or call attention to herself. If she were to make eye contact with any of her sister's sworn enemies, she would give them a faint smile and try to avoid confrontation if at all possible. Some days, of course, were better than others.

"Hey, twin," Shannon hissed with a hint of nastiness she was infamously known for.

"Hello, Shannon," replied London nonchalantly, trying not to look up. She knew both Kenya and Shannon equally hated each other and that made Shannon in turn hate London because she looked exactly like her sister. *All this crap probably over some stupid boy,* thought London. "Why are females so one-dimensional? They need to elevate their brains," she mumbled underneath her breath.

"Excuse me, but did you say something over there you want to repeat, Ms. Thang?" growled Shannon as she bucked her eyes out wanting trouble.

Having more self-control than her sister, London shook her head and walked away, not once looking back. She heard Shannon and her girls still laughing as she made her way down the hall but she didn't care. London scurried up the hallway quickly before the last bell rang, not wanting to be late. As she passed by one of the class-rooms, she saw the most popular girl in the entire school surrounded by a flock of boys. She waved at her sister, Kenya, who waved back. London had to get to class. The bell was ringing.

Chapter Three

Bitch, Please!

After three grueling years of high school passed, it was the last week of the term. The twins had made it and were going to finally be seniors next semester. The only thing left before vacation was final exams. Kenya acted as if passing them would be a total breeze. Concentrating on tests wasn't easy for Kenya. The popular teen knew that she needed to study but would still sneak out of the house almost every night doing God knows what with God knows who. London, on the other hand, would study constantly, keeping her head buried in the books. Although they were both smart girls when it came down to it, unfortunately only London would apply herself.

Gran often worried about both her granddaughters' well-being. However, there was only so much she could do or say to point them in the right direction. At some point it would be up to the sisters themselves to make the right decisions and choices in general. The flow of life was starting to take its toll on Gran; she was getting old. In between the grief of losing both of her own children and trying her best to raise two now-teenage girls, she was rapidly losing speed.

The last bell rang and it was thankfully over. The final class for the semester had concluded. Rambunctious and excited student after student poured out the doors of the school building like it was on fire and they had on gasoline attire. The joy of no more class until fall was on their minds, but the true source of their merriment was the anticipation that'd been growing all day, really all year long. Kenya and Shannon, constant adversaries who argued day after day, were about to battle and the shit was about to be on. They were going to fight on the basketball court after school. Everyone knew about it, even the teachers. But they didn't give a shit; their so-called tour of duty was finally over, so to hell with the students and their madness!

"Let them kill each other," London overheard one of the teachers snarl while she drank her coffee. "Their parents are raising little animals so this is the type of behavior I expect."

Walking past, London, who was ear hustling, couldn't help herself and jumped into the otherwise private conversation. "Wow, you're supposed to be adults, teachers no less. We should be looking to you for guidance. You should be trying to find a way to help us end this black-on-black crime instead of turning a deaf ear." London was in rare form as she waited for a sign of remorse from the teacher. "Somebody should report y'all!"

"Well, Li'l Miss Wannabe Harriet Tubman and Oprah rolled into one," the younger of the teachers smugly responded to the teen. "Instead of you being all up in here giving us a black history lesson, don't you think you should be out on that basketball court trying to stop your sister from getting her pretty little teeth stumped out her mouth?" The teacher, not trying to defend her initial proclamation, was rolling her head around and snapping her fingers, just like she was London's equal. "You're in here judging us like your parents weren't out in the streets back in the day destroying the minds of the youth! Girl, bye! We all know the story of your people!"

Hearing her sarcastic statement about her deceased parents and Kenya's impending battle swiftly snatched London back into reality of what was really about to take place. It was true. While she was preoccupied inside being a one-woman martyr for humanity, the here and now was taking place just yards away. She had to get off her soapbox and get outside fast. That no-good, "always got something ugly to say about folk" Shannon had been running off at the mouth all day long about how she was gonna jump on Kenya when school was out. Well, seeing how the last bell had rung over ten minutes prior, London knew time was ticking. "I hate violence, but there's no way I'm not gonna have my sister's back," London said out loud as she ran down the deserted hallway, bolting out of the school's double doors. Immediately eyeing the crowd gathering, swarming around like flies on a pile of shit on the basketball court, London couldn't believe how many people were actually cheering, happy to see two females try to beat one another down. *Why can't Kenya stay out of trouble for once?* she thought, quickly approaching the middle of all the commotion in the field. *It seems like Gran is right. Her temper is gonna get her in big trouble one day!*

"Fake ass!" Shannon brazenly taunted, feeling as if the crowd was backing her up. With her hands on her hips, she was front and center of the small mob surrounded by her so-called clique, which consisted of three ghetto-painted-face females who also took the bus from the projects every day to get to school. However, that didn't mean much of nothing to Kenya at all. Matter of fact, the only thing it really meant was they weren't just hood rats; they were low-budget project rats. To Kenya it didn't matter much if you were rich, poor, black, or white, old, young, boy, or girl. If you came for her, she had no problem whatsoever returning the favor ten times over and coming for you. So if Shannon wanted to feel Kenya's wrath, then so be it, she would. It was on.

"What?" Kenya let her intended victim rant and rave before she had her turn at showing Shannon what was really good in the hood.

"You heard me, bitch! What it do, Ms. Uppity? You been acting like you wanted some all year long, so what's up?" Shannon was straight-up frontin'. Honestly she was scared to death, but she tried her best to not let it show, especially in front of half the student body.

The crowd was geeking it up and that's all Kenya, already mentally prepared to take her opponent's head off, needed to hear. Knowing her DNA bloodline ran deep on her father's side, Kenya didn't crack a smile, showing not one tooth. She was cut from a different cloth than many, and, in her words, they didn't even make that fabric anymore. The west side's known wild child offspring of Johnnie and Melinda Roberts did her best clowning in front of an audience and this was one of her biggest to date. She had a point to prove about hoes running off at the mouth just because they had lips, and school was back in session for Shannon.

Carmen was on her left and London, not truly wanting to fight but would and could, had just burst through the crowd and was loyally posted on her right. Allan, who'd dropped out a couple years back, was also up at the school to hold them down, just in case one of those busters Shannon would trick with flexed and wanted their ass kicked too.

"Fake ass? Come on now seriously, is that what you let rip out that raggedy grill mouth? Girl, look at you, from the bottom to the top you need a clue. Your synthetic weave has been recycled from week to week. Your blouse got a permanent ring around the collar and do your pants even know what an iron is?" Kenya was going ham and the mesmerized crowd loved the show she was giving them.

Some of the guys in the bunch were ashamed that they ever kicked it with Shannon let alone spent some loose change on her. London felt bad for her also, but deep down inside she knew she had it coming. Yet, at that moment, no one felt as bad as Shannon, who had no defense for the slaughter. Her girls had eased away and faded back into the background. It was obvious they didn't want any of the verbal beat down their so-called homegirl was getting, who was staring down at the ground with tears starting to form in her eyes.

"Oh hell naw, you stankin' trash bucket! Why you got your head down now? With them ran-over shoes! Did you walk over here from Africa?" Kenya still never cracked a smile as she twisted up her face. The girl was cold-blooded, just like her daddy, and wouldn't stop going until she was satisfied in totally humiliating Shannon. "You want it with me for real? Girl, you better get your life!"

Most of the students standing around were almost in tears from the entertainment Kenya was providing. Carmen was begging her best friend to stop running Shannon's name through the mud because her side was beginning to hurt. She, like the many other spectators, just couldn't stop laughing at Shannon's expense. London, cut from the same cloth as her sister on the other hand, was just like her twin, not cracking a smile either. She knew Kenya much better than anyone else and could tell that the girl had "blood in her eyes." *Poor Shannon,* was all she could think at that point.

"All bullshit aside let's tear this court up," Kenya, aggravated, spoke in a cold, callous tone, following her taunting words with a sock dead to Shannon's jaw, who just stood there, speechless, holding her face.

Just then, luckily for Shannon, the school security arrived, breaking up their one-sided battle before things grew worse. The crowd slowly dispersed, including the twins and their friends. As they made their way down Linwood Avenue, Carmen and Allan couldn't stop making jokes about what had just jumped off. They both were taking turns pretending to be Shannon. Even the normally quiet Amber was cracking up. Hell, she and London had been on the receiving end of Shannon's insults time and time again. It felt good to see the bully get a small taste of her own medicine for once.

While the others went on with the jokes, finally going their separate ways, London walked alongside her sister. She placed her hand on Kenya's shoulder, attempting to calm her down. When Kenya got heated, it was hard for her to let stuff go. Luckily, the sisters finally made it to their house without any further incidents. Kenya sat down on the concrete stair and London followed. As soon as they looked at one another they both burst out laughing.

"Dang, girl, you really let her have it. I was trying hard as heck not to laugh all in her face." London giggled. "But she deserved every bit of it. She's a bully!"

Kenya couldn't wait to roast her sister. "What about you? You came bursting all through the crowd like Freddy fucking Krueger! Shiiit, you even scared me."

In the midst of all of the laughter, they didn't even notice Gran pulling in the driveway.

"Hey, Gran!" London yelled out, running off the porch to help her grandmother with her bags.

"Hey, baby, how are you and how was school?" Gran hugged London tightly.

"It was the best day of the entire year!"

Kenya, acting out of character, cut in, actually hugging Gran too. They all walked to the porch arm in arm, smiling. Today they were a happy family, even Kenya, who was for once not being a pain. It's surprising what an ass kicking would do, especially when it's not your ass that got kicked.

Chapter Four

Seniors

"Summer came and went so quickly. I can't wait. We're finally seniors! I hope we have a few new teachers, maybe someone to teach English or math." London was going on and on for what seemed like forever. She loved school, even if it was Central High.

"New teachers, forget all that! Girl, we're seniors now, queens of the school! It's our turn to be running thangs up in there. It's gonna be a new sheriff in that motherfucker!" Kenya was too excited also as she thought about her impending spot as HBIC of the school. She was spinning around with her hands in the air. "I can't wait!" Kenya was cheesin' from ear to ear.

The girls had become a lot closer during the summer months. Gran had suffered a mild heart attack while she was at work and had to stay in the hospital for almost two weeks straight. The twins had to rely on each other much more for everything from moral support to sharing the responsibility of the household. It was then, even more than before, that they learned of the special bond the two shared. A little bit of maturity on both their behalves had settled in. If they ran into a problem, London figured out the solution and Kenya executed the plan, putting it in motion. They now woke up daily on their own and instead of Gran making them breakfast they in turn would cook for her. While the twins still hung out with their old friends at school, for the first time in three years they walked to Central together. Sometimes it was Linwood Avenue, and others it would be the side streets.

As the months started to go by and the seasons changed, so did Kenya. She just couldn't help herself. As much as she was fighting her alter ego, she'd unfortunately slipped back into her old, wild, carefree ways she was so infamous for. School and turning in homework assignments on time had once again become a second priority in her young, reckless life. All of Kenya's grades she struggled so feverishly to get up to par were rapidly falling, and lastly she returned to skipping class most of the time. She was heading downhill rapidly and nothing anyone said or did could seem to slow her intentions of being "not shit" down.

London, disgusted at what she was watching take place and couldn't stop, blamed her sister's spiral on that stupid foolish-oriented boyfriend of Kenya's. London knew Ty was nothing more than a car thief clown who had dropped out of school in tenth grade and ran the streets of Detroit on a nickel-and-dime adventure trying to sell drugs for the next man when he could get put on. Like most young dudes in their neighborhood, he wasn't smart enough or had enough game to have his own sack to risk getting knocked and going to jail for; he hustled to make the next nigga's pockets fat. Ty, in all his ill-witted wisdom, was always busy putting different kinds of dumb, idiotic ideas in Kenya's gullible mind. Kenya always had delusions of grandeur and escaping hood life no matter how she could do it, hook or crook. Engulfed by nothing but getting off Glendale Street and out of Gran's strict and spiritual household, Kenya was starting to cut off everyone in her small circle of friends, even Allan and Carmen. At night she was either on the phone plotting the demise of her current lifestyle situation or sneaking out of the house to meet up with Ty.

"Hey, boo, it's me, baby," whispered Kenya as quietly as she could. "I can't talk long. My sister is bugging out on me about my grades so I gotta at least do some of my homework."

"Why she be all actin' like a book gonna help you eat out in these streets? She needs to be trying to hook up with my boy. You know for some reason he dig her plain-Jane ass! Plus he's paid, I ain't bullshitting!" Ty cleared his throat after choking on some Kush. "He be pulling in major ends almost every day with these hot box cars we been getting off this lot and he got a sack of this good shit I'm blowing on." He coughed once more. "For real, Kenya, seriously your sister needs to wise the fuck up and get some of this bread from ol' boy!"

Kenya was beginning to get irritated and annoyed with his conversation and the disrespectful direction it was taking. After it was all done and said, that was her twin sister he was badmouthing and tripping on. Since she had an emotional attachment to him, Kenya didn't pay much attention when he talked shit about her—she could overlook that for the sake of young puppy love—but fuck him dogging London just because he thought he could. He was going too far with his comments and suggestions and she wasn't trying to hear any more of it.

"Listen, Ty, I already done told you I was on the clock with talking to you in the first damn place! Now I got a bright idea for your dropout-ass to process: why don't you stop riding your boy's nut sack so hard, leave my sister's name out your mouth, and show me some fucking attention? How about that, nigga?" Kenya twisted her face up as she spoke each word like she meant it, and of course she did.

Ty, who always thought much more of himself than anyone else ever did, immediately got caught in his feelings, wasting no time going ham. "You know what?

Fuck you, Kenya, and your stuck-up-ass ugly sister. I was trying to turn both you bitches on to some real game, but I see once again your ho ass ain't trying to respect my gangster!"

Before Kenya had a chance to respond to that lame-ass bullshit knowledge he was kicking, he'd already slammed the phone down, hanging up on her. She couldn't help but laugh. True enough Ty was her so-called man, so to speak, but he also was a little punk and just about everyone on the west side knew it. He was scared of his own shadow and here he was trying to go for bad.

Whenever they were at the mall or out to the park, he would always stand mute when this guy or that guy tried to push up on Kenya. Later on when she would ask him how come he ain't say shit, he would make up excuses and try to play that shit off like he wasn't low-key terrified of getting his ass handed to him on a platter. Kenya started to think, *Why isn't he just honest with me and himself and speak the truth? He could have just simply said, "Damn, baby, you know I ain't say shit back to them cats 'cause I'm a coward and was scared that nigga was gonna chin check me."*

She almost fell on the floor from laughing so hard at the sheer thought. Tears were rolling down her cheeks from thinking about that entire crazy scenario playing itself out. He'd call back tomorrow, begging as usual. He always did. "Different day, same idiot," she said out loud. When she finally looked up, Kenya saw her sister looking at her, shaking her head.

"I hope that you're still laughing when you get your grades at the end of this semester," nagged London in a maternal tone.

Kenya opted not to let her sister in on the joke she found so hilarious. "Yes, Mom, I got you. I'm about to hit the books now."

***

The school year seemed to drag on for what seemed like forever and a day. Ironically both girls were growing bored with school and what it had to offer. London, the smartest book-wise, had received the highest GPA semester after semester. She was top of her class in every honor class they offered and that still was not enough to challenge her brain. The devoted scholar often let her mind roam about what the next year would be about and how college campus life would be. London was more than ready to graduate and leave for the university of her choice on a full scholarship. Most of her teachers were incompetent in her eyes and were going to be happy to see her cross that stage. London had this thing for correcting the teachers so much they should have paid her to teach the class. There was no question, hands down, as to who the valedictorian would be that school year: Ms. Amia London Roberts.

Meanwhile, on the other hand, Ms. Amoya Kenya Roberts was also making a name for herself at Central High School. Of course, the self-proclaimed diva was named both homecoming queen and prom queen. That was expected because she was always fly and sociable with her peers. Not to mention after all the flirting she did, every boy at school voted for her, hoping for a date or at least the attention she gave them during the election process. Kenya was also voted "class smile," "class legs," "class body," and what shocked even Kenya was that she, not her academically industrious twin London, was voted most likely to succeed! However, the question that swam in London's mind was, *Succeed at what?*

Chapter Five

Farewells

Graduation day had finally arrived and both of the girls were dressed to kill. The girls' uncle had taken both of them on a shopping spree to New York to get them gear to look perfect for their special day. The twins respectfully had on pink Armani tailored cut suits. The buttons were gold and trimmed in the same pink that was in the fabric. They each had open-toed gator sandals with a small heel on them. London and Kenya, for the first time since they were small children, wore their hair in the exact same style. It was in a French roll tightly tucked with soft sandy-brown curls cascading down across the sides of their faces. Each had also gotten their nails manicured and a pedicure the day before.

Gran, proud as any grandmother could be, had let them sleep in an extra thirty minutes while she made them a breakfast fit for a queen. Lovingly, she helped London get dressed and ready, and tried her best to keep an always-hyper Kenya still. The girls then left Gran at home to get herself together for one of the biggest days of all of their lives.

"I love you two very, very much and I'll see you at the school. I'm proud of you both and promise me you'll never ever forget that." Gran hugged both of her grandchildren tightly and kissed them, before letting the two leave out the door.

The twins made their grand entrance into the packed auditorium, and all eyes were definitely on them. Both were getting mad crazy attention. Everyone, students, teachers, and counselors were all confused as to which twin was London and which twin was Kenya. The girls, each being who they were meant to be, quickly removed all doubt when they opened their mouths and began to speak. That was always a dead giveaway with the twins.

Kenya was loud and off the chain and her sister was noticeably quiet when it came to anything other than schoolwork. London was more than a little nervous about the speech she was slated to deliver. She had worked hard all four years and rightly deserved to be rewarded standing behind that podium. All of the late nights she spent lying awake reading and the days she stayed in the house studying were all getting ready to pay off for her. London was proud of herself. She had a wide smile plastered on her face and a nervousness shaking inside. The dedicated teen knew her next step was college, then acquiring a degree, making all her dreams come true.

All the graduating seniors scrambled around posing for pictures with their classmates and parents and signing yearbooks. Kenya, vain as always, broke free from the excited, energized crowd, posting up in front of the wall-length mirror backstage. Turning from side to side, she kept adjusting her cap and checking her makeup. There was no one in the world Kenya admired more than herself. She was stuck on herself and knew that she was a straight-up dime. She was feeling herself, even in a cap and gown.

The girls' uncle, his girlfriend, and a few of their distant cousins were seated in the far back row. The twins weren't cordial with their cousins at all. In fact, they barely spoke to them even if they saw each other in passing inside the mall. The girls knew their uncle probably had to strong-arm them into coming to represent, but they really didn't care if they were there one way or another. Everyone, their uncle included, was a sidebar to them today. The twins had saved Gran, the most important person in both their lives, a seat front and center. With love, respect, and devotion they placed two single pink roses on it for her. Gran had fought hard and sacrificed a lot to get them to this point. They wanted her to know when she arrived in the auditorium that this was her day also.

Time was ticking. It was close to eleven o'clock and the principal was yelling for everyone to get in line so that they could march in and begin the sure-to-be long, drawn-out commencement ceremony. It was time to start what the entire senior class had been anticipating for four years ever since they were freshmen.

"I still don't see her, do you?" London held her sister's hand, shaking, still extremely nervous about giving a speech in front of all the boisterous people.

"No, but you know Gran. She probably couldn't find the right outfit to wear." Kenya chuckled while trying to conceal her equal worry for their grandmother's tardiness.

Everyone backstage was hyped, anxious to get underway; however, the girls continued to peek out from behind the burgundy and gold curtains every few seconds, but still no Gran. Trying to find excuses for her absence, each started to think of what could be possibly keeping her, especially on this day.

"The telephone must have rung and, you know Gran, she was probably too polite to rush one of her church lady friends having a problem off the phone. She's almost here, I bet." London shrugged her shoulders. She was almost in tears.

Kenya continued to hold her sister's hand trying her absolute best to calm London down. Little did the distraught twins know that at that very moment in time the phone did ring. Sadly it was God and He had decided to call Gran home. Up in age, the devoted mother and grandmother never completely recovered from the heart attack that she'd suffered the previous year. With the determination of a lion, the elderly God-fearing senior citizen's weak heart barely held on until London and Kenya were both grown. Gran fought a hard fight but was truly tired.

"Ms. Roberts and Ms. Roberts would you two like to join the rest of us, so that we may begin?" snarled the frazzled-minded principal. He was running around on edge trying to stay on schedule but it was not happening. The girls peeked out in the crowd one last time before the ceremony started. They were still holding hands. They both still felt uneasy.

"Well, this is it," they both said in unison, staring at one another for comfort and moral support while each wondered where Gran was at.

"I love you, London."

"I love you too, Kenya."

"*Say U Promise!*" They each laughed as they dropped hands.

Kenya walked over to the line that was forming and took her spot in line with the other Rs; and London, of course, took her place on stage so that she could make her speech and receive her honors scholarships declarations and hard-earned certificates of merit. The girls smiled at each other from opposite sides of the room. They were overjoyed at the occasion, but solemnly knew this would be the beginning of being their own individual selves, not a twin, as they had been since conception. As the ceremony started each twin wondered constantly throughout, *Where is Gran?*

***

A day filled with the extreme promise of the future was also a day filled with sadness for the twins. They had struggled relentlessly through guest speakers, awards, and the seemingly endless roll call of the senior graduates, and still no Gran. Dry mouthed, London could barely get through her speech without stumbling over the same words repeatedly that she had practiced for weeks. The haunting sight of Gran's empty seat with the two pink roses lying alone on the chair made her nauseated and sick to her stomach.

At the end of the ceremony, the girls weren't interested in taking pictures. They had no desire to hug everyone and pretend like they would really miss one another. All of the crowd fanfare was of no consequence to either of them. No sooner than they found their uncle did they jump in his SUV and make him drive them home as quickly as possible. They pulled up in the driveway and before the truck could come to a complete stop the two were jumping out and running up toward the door.

When the Kenya and London got the door unlocked, they bolted inside. That's when they received the pain of ten lifetimes combined. They laid eyes on Gran. She was fully dressed and sitting back in her favorite chair. There were two letters lying in her lap. Each had one of the girls' names written on the white envelope.

After all the initial pandemonium broke loose and the paramedics, police, and the morgue had left with the body, each twin, feeling totally lost and in denial, sat quietly in a daze halfway reading the letters their beloved Gran had written. The letters told each of them to always trust, depend on, and rely on one other no matter what the circumstances would be.

Both of the twins wept uncontrollably at Gran's Home Going Service, even having to be ushered out to get some air and a chance to recompose themselves. Gran in all her glory truly looked like an angel. The sometimes-tormented, but always-spiritual loyal woman was finally at peace. She'd left the house fifty-fifty jointly to both London and Kenya. Each girl would receive two acres of land down South in Jackson, Alabama. That was where their grandmother and mother were originally born before relocating to Detroit. They also were to receive $20,000 each in life insurance money. Gran, loving her girls to the end, made sure each would have a fair start at life.

It had been a little more than two and a half months since Gran had gone and London and Kenya often spent nights lying awake missing her in their own special way. September rolled around quickly and London, who had wrestled with the idea of accepting the scholarship from State University, was getting ready for college. Sure the school was also located in Michigan, but it was up north. It was almost a two hour car ride from home, and away from Kenya, her twin. London would have to stay on campus which meant she couldn't keep tabs on her often out-of-control sister. Miss Kenya, now living with a little bit of pocket money and no real adult supervision, had gotten a little wild and untamable, to say the least. Yet, despite her shortcomings, and most, if not all, of Kenya's recent decisions and behavior, London could hardly fathom being apart from her.

"I've got to do this. I've worked much too hard not to push on." London was talking to Gran's picture as she packed it in her bag.

Amber somberly came over to help her best friend pack. She was going to miss her homegirl and confidante. "Dang, I wish I was going with you, so that way we could both get out this tired hood. You are so lucky."

"I wished you were going too, so I wouldn't be so lonely up there with all those strangers."

Both Amber and London looked at each other and sighed. Amber, not the smartest person London knew, barely graduated and felt like in all probability she would forever be stuck working in the beauty supply on Dexter Boulevard. They sadly exchanged their good-byes and Amber left, heading up toward Dexter to work.

Everything was all packed and London's uncle was on the way with his pickup truck. As she sat on the front stairs looking around at her surroundings, trying to remember all the flowers and rocks in the street, London closed her eyes. She wanted to make sure she didn't forget the neighborhood. Squeezing them tightly shut, she locked the memory in her brain. London would miss the hood and all the foolish antics that went along with living in it. Crime infested or not, it was her home, and no matter where she went, who she met, or what great things in life she ever accomplished, she'd never forget where she came from or the ethics Gran had instilled in her. Opening her eyes, she soon heard the blasting sounds of jazz music coming down the street and London knew that it had to be her uncle.

Damn near pulling the truck up on the porch with the huge rimmed tires he jumped out. "Hey, baby girl." He beamed with pride of where they were headed and what London was sure to succeed in. "You's about ready to go get this family some higher learning going on or what?" He grabbed London off her feet and started swinging her around. He was so proud of her; everyone who knew Gran was.

"Dang, Uncle, I can hardly breathe, put me down!" she begged as her feet dangled trying to touch the ground.

"Okay, baby girl! Are you all packed? Do you have enough clothes? Do you need to go get more supplies?" He was talking so fast, on a ten, that London had to tell him to calm down.

"Yes, I'm fine, so don't worry." She playfully pushed his arm, smiling. "I have everything I need and what I don't have I can buy up there in the next few days, so stop worrying about me. I'm gonna be good. I promise!"

London had a full ride scholarship: room, board, and books completely paid for. Whatever else London would need, she could easily take from the money that Gran had left to her. Unlike Kenya, she'd saved more than the majority of the life insurance money that Gran blessed her and her sister with. She'd basically purchased a laptop, a new cell phone, some much-needed and wanted books, and banked the rest for the future.

"Well, London, where is your sister?" her uncle suspiciously questioned. "Why ain't her fast, wannabe-grown-ass out on this porch helping you with your stuff?"

No sooner, seemingly seconds, had the words left out his mouth, than they heard the annoying screech of tires turn the corner. Uncle, instinctively from living the street life, reached under his shirt and put his hand on his thriller. He didn't know who was coming down the block driving like a bat outta hell, yet he did know that any clown-ass fool who wanted to get his "big shot on" was gonna catch a few hot ones real quick, fast, and in a hurry. As the car finally came into focus, he and London both shared an expression of disgust. It was Kenya, riding with that foul-ass Ty, nine outta ten in a stolen vehicle.

"Hey, y'all! What up, doe?" Kenya, obviously turned up, jumped out the car looking like who did it and why. Her hair was out of place and her clothes were slightly wrinkled, looking as if she had slept in them.

"What the fuck is your problem?" Uncle never raised his voice or even cursed in front of his nieces, but he had been pushed to his limit and was pissed off. "You look one hot mess! Have you lost your damn mind out here or what?"

London got terrified not knowing what her uncle was going to do, knowing his reputation for violence, but not Kenya. She was didn't give a shit what he or anyone had to say about what she did or who she did it with. Not even blinking, she stood tall in her uncle's face ready for whatever. She had that Roberts blood pumping through her veins just like her uncle and his brother, her daddy, did and Kenya feared no man or woman for that matter. Maybe it was that fat blunt that she had for breakfast or the wine from the night before still circulating in her system giving her liquid courage, but whatever it was she started to laugh.

Ty, terrified as his girl's uncle noticed the ignition column of the car broken and a screwdriver on seat, knew better than to try to go up against the seasoned criminal everyone knew was a cold-blooded killer if need be. He wised up real fast and peeled away from the curb as quickly as he had pulled up, leaving Kenya to face her own demons so to speak. Ty knew the twins' uncle only by his ruthless reputation on the streets and knew he wasn't for any foolishness, so he couldn't help but exhale as he made it down the block to the stop sign without a bullet in the back of his head.

"Have you been out all damn night with that lowlife car-stealing bastard?" The twins' uncle roughly grabbed Kenya by her shirt, waiting for an answer.

Kenya's defiant laughter quickly turned into pure shock as he lifted her upward. "Let me go, let me go!" she cried as she tried unsuccessfully to snatch away from his strong grip.

"Listen, little girl! I don't give a sweet fuck how grown you running around here pretending you are! Let's get this straight. I'll kill you dead first and anyone else who tries to lead your ass down the wrong path. Do you fucking understand me, Kenya?" Their uncle was furious as the veins started to jump out the side of his neck.

London, desperate to not have any trouble, came in between two of the only people she truly called family and began crying. "Please don't do this, please. Not on my last day here," she continuously pleaded.

Seeing both of his nieces in tears made their uncle's rage slightly soften, but it was obviously his sentiment, for what he'd told Kenya remained the same and by the evil side eye he gave her she knew to take heed. "Come on, London, let's get your stuff loaded and get going." He grabbed the last few items off the porch and got back in his truck without so much as glancing in Kenya's general direction at all.

"Well, sis, this is it. I'm gonna miss you, Kenya."

"I'm gonna miss you too. First Mom and Pops, then Gran, and now you, but I ain't tripping." Kenya tried to force a smile as her heart broke. "I'll be good holding it down."

"Kenya, I'm only a phone call away. Matter of fact, I'll call you as soon as I get there." They hugged each other as the tears continued to flow.

"If you need me," they both said at the same time like twins often did.

"One love." London smiled.

"*Say U Promise*," chanted Kenya.

London jumped in the truck and the girls kept their eyes glued to the other one until the truck turned off the block, heading upstate.

Chapter Six

London

Even though they'd left early in the day, after eating lunch it was getting dark by the time they reached the campus. Understandably, London also had to go and say good-bye to all of the neighbors she had grown to love over the years. She had stopped by Gran's church and thanked everyone for the money that they had collected for her sendoff. London told them that she didn't need it, but the congregation wasn't trying to hear that. Her grandmother had helped each and every last one of them and their families. So their giving what little bit they collected was all in love.

Overwhelmed, London took a good look around the campus as they drove up. "Wow, it's a lot bigger than what I remember from my visit on the tour we took in our senior year." Taking out a small pack of papers, she was puzzled. "Well, I know I'm supposed to be in Davis Hall dormitory. So let's see . . ."

They followed all the signs posted along the side of each twisted street corner. When finally they found the building, London leaped out the truck and jogged up to the double glass door. As she entered, she saw plenty of new, interesting faces milling around looking just as confused as she was. After standing in a long line at the front desk, it was her turn to give the lady her personal information.

"Hello, I'm Amia London Roberts. I'm trying to check in."

The young lady behind the desk punched her name into the computer and retrieved London's keys, room assignment, and some important information booklets that would make her transition into college life easier. Keys in hand and a huge smile on her face, London skipped back out to the truck, telling her uncle that they could pull around the back entrance of the building and unload. In the company of at least ten other excited families, the pair patiently waited until it was their turn to use the big freight elevator.

"All right then, baby girl, let's get you settled in."

Her uncle was in a much better mood than earlier when he'd had that big blowout confrontation with Kenya, and London was glad. One half of the elated twins started to grab her things up in her arms, placing them on the elevator as other cars, trucks, and vans pulled up, waiting their turns. *He is the best uncle in the world. Thank God he has my back!* London lovingly thought as they carried load after load up to her new dorm room.

After they were finally done, her uncle started to get a sad expression on his face. "I'm gonna miss you, baby girl. I want you to represent for the entire family. Your father and mother would be so proud of you if they were here!" He fought back the tears thinking about his dead brother and the circumstances of his death. "I'll know you'll be the smartest one here. We're all counting on you."

"Don't worry, Uncle, I won't let you down. I don't know about being the smartest, but I promise I'll study hard and do my very best." London hugged him tightly and before he left out the dorm room door, he reached in his pocket, blessing her with five one hundred dollar bills.

"Uncle, I'm fine. Seriously, I have enough money to get by," she pleaded as she backed away from his extended hand.

"Okay, London, dig this here. I'm gonna tell you what your daddy always told me: as long as you black, you don't have enough money. Now take this and put it up for later!" He then forced the money into her hand, refusing to take no for an answer.

London smiled and told him that she loved him while they both emotionally fought back the tears.

As he was leaving, London's new roommate, unbeknownst to him, was making her way down the long hallway. The struggle she was having was real. The young teen was having trouble with all the bags and boxes that she was attempting to carry and kick down the hallway by herself. Unfortunately many of her belongings were falling out of her arms and onto the floor.

"Dang why did I bring so much damn stuff?" she spoke out loud, not caring who might have overheard her talking to herself.

"Maybe because a real woman needs a lot of personal items to make strange places feel more like home. How about that?" London's uncle beamed as he bent down to help the overdeveloped young girl gather together her things.

"Wow, thank you so much, sir." She smiled and picked up the bag she was carrying, throwing it back over her shoulder. "I'm just down the hallway I think."

As she watched the numbers getting higher and higher, London's uncle, being a man, watched her body and the way it moved like a hawk. *Damn, I need to go back to school!* He couldn't do shit but shake his head as his manhood automatically jumped.

"Hey, this is it here!" Fatima yelled as they burst through the door that was still cracked open. "I made it."

London, who was unpacking, turned around and saw her uncle standing in the doorway with a huge grin on his face.

"Hey, girl! I'm Fatima James, your new roommate." Out of breath she dropped all her things on the floor and blew up in the air.

"Hello, Fatima, I'm Amia Roberts, but please call me London." The two gave each other a short brief hug. "Oh, and I see that you must have met my uncle."

"Your uncle? Well yes, I guess did, well sort of." Fatima started to trip over her words as she noticed just how handsome her knight in shining armor really was under the bright room lights.

Knowing he had caught the young girl's eye, he reached back inside his pocket, peeling London off another hundred from his rubber-banded stack. "Well, ladies, I guess I'll leave you two to unpack and get to know each other." Of course, he made sure that Fatima was watching as he strutted his older self back toward the door. "Put some snacks in the fridge for both of you." He then winked his eye at his niece and blew a kiss at Fatima.

"We will. Bye, Uncle. Have a safe trip back!" London was almost speechless by her uncle's blatant flirting with her roommate.

The girls started pulling different stuff out of their boxes and bags to add their own individual personal touches and own flair to the room. While London's side of the room had a lot of pictures of her small family, which consisted of Gran, Kenya, and her uncle, reference books, notebooks, and a few stuffed animals, Fatima had snapshots of Africa and pictures of her Muslim parents in various racial and religious freedom marches they had taken part in. Fatima also had a lot of bumper stickers bearing black pride slogans and tons of books about African Americans. London naturally wondered why Fatima didn't choose to attend an all-black school since she was obviously pro-black.

"Wow, you sure have a lot of books. It's like you have your very own library." London flipped though all of the various titles, somewhat in awe of Fatima's interest.

"Yeah, girl, I love me some books. I stay up hours reading." Fatima smiled at her new roommate. The girls knew, right then and there, they would grow to be good friends. "Hey, I am starving. Let's get something to eat. And then we can check out the campus at the same time." Fatima rubbed on her empty stomach.

London eagerly agreed with her roommate. "Okay, but let me try to call my sister first and let her know that I made it here safely." She reached in a box and handed Fatima a picture of Kenya. "This was taken at the park this summer."

"Damn, this is your sister? You're a twin? Girl, I thought that these other pictures were of you at the club or something with your hair down and makeup on!" Fatima couldn't believe they were two different people. Fatima smiled at London. "Go ahead, girl, and make your call to your alter ego. I'll be down in the lobby."

London picked up the phone, dialing home.

Kenya

Kenya slowly walked up the stairs looking back one last time as she saw her uncle and sister fade out of sight. She put her key in the door and started to make her way into the empty, sure-to-be lonely house. Stopping in front of the mirror in the front hallway, she took a good, long look at herself. "Well, it's just you and me now. It's time to do you, get your shit together, and hold yourself down." Kenya said it over and over out loud as if she was trying to convince herself of it being true. Taking a deep breath, she had to smile thinking about London and all she did to make both their lives better since Gran's passing. The house was clean as a whistle and smelled like it had been scrubbed top to bottom. London, thankfully, had washed all of the dishes and skillets, cleaned the carpet, and washed all of her sister's "dirty for weeks on end" clothes. London always knew that housework was never really Kenya's thing and had hooked her up one last time before going off to school. *Good lookin', sis.* Kenya nodded as she passed by London's graduation picture that was sitting on the mantle next to her own.

Tired from partying from the night before and not having much else to do, Kenya went over to the new couch she'd bought and fell across it, feet in the air. She then reached for the remote to her high-definition plasma television that she'd had mounted on the living room wall. It had so many buttons on that damn remote it would take a brain scientist, let alone Kenya, a year to learn how to use them all. Kenya, almost penniless, against London's advice, had used most of her insurance money Gran left her to freak the house out. It looked like a magazine layout. In between all the mall shopping and a used car that was on its last leg already, the wannabe hood diva was damn near broke.

At this point, especially considering what had just taken place, Kenya knew that she had all but cut herself out of her uncle's bottomless pockets. Luckily the household bills were paid up for a month or so, but Kenya realized she had to get on that money trail and make a few things happen if she wanted to continue to floss wherever she stepped out to.

Never outside the hustle loop for long, Kenya already put up on a quick way to make some fast, easy cash in hand. Ty, with all his schemes and scams, claimed to have the inside hookup, so why the hell not! Shit, she wasn't slow to the game by a long shot, but stripping? Kenya thought about it as she stared at her checkbook that was a few zeros from balancing out. Heads Up was the hottest strip joint up in the D. Everyone knew that it was the spot where real playas would meet and greet. It was no big secret that there was nothing but wall-to-wall loot in that motherfucker, and girls not half as pretty as Kenya, some not built like shit, getting paid out the ass. From flashy hustlers and blue-collar factory workers to plain-style fucking trick-ass niggas from around the way, they all knew that they had to come correct with their paper game to even walk through the doors of Heads Up, not to mention hanging out in the VIP. That was a given, flat out.

Kenya, trying to get in the zone, switched to the uncut video channel on cable and turned the surround sound up on double bump. "Fuck that shit!" She was hyped as she moved around the room as if she was the star of the evening. "I can do all those dances and make my ass bounce too." She pranced in the mirror and turned around to watch that motherfucker move. "I'm the shit, fuck 'em hoes! They can eat shit and die! I'm gonna make my ends up in that place as soon as I get my foot in the door!"

Exhausted from performing for herself, Kenya started to run her bathwater while she continued to get her dance on. When the water was just right, Kenya slowly undressed and eased her sweaty-ass into the hot, bubble-filled tub. Kenya, trying to get turned up as she daydreamed about her new desired profession, lit her blunt of Kush and lay back. *I guess I can call Ty's ho-ass tomorrow and see what's really good with Heads Up.* Lost in her thoughts as she listened to the music still echoing off the walls and got buzzed, the house phone rang twice as she was soaking. "Fuck whoever it is," she mumbled, blowing smoke rings into the air. "I'm chillin' the most."

Kenya, caught up in her own new world, had missed her twin sister's call.

London

"Hey, girl, let's go." London found Fatima talking to a group of other students who also lived in the dorm. They all introduced themselves and talked for a minute or two.

Fatima, having had just met her roommate, could easily tell by the look on London's face that something was wrong. Without reservation, she questioned London. "What's the deal, black girl? Is everything all good on the home front?"

"Naw, nothing much is wrong. I was just wondering where my sister is, that's all. She didn't answer the phone." London then got it in her head that she had to stop worrying so much about Kenya and let her live her life. After all, from this point on she wouldn't be there every day to watch over her. "Hey, girl, come on. I'm hungry, let's roll out." London changed her expression and attitude, while trying to sound cool. "She'll call when she calls!"

The pair of new roomies left the dorm, laughing and joking all the way to a twenty-four-hour greasy spoon on the edge of campus that some of the other students, all upperclassmen, had told Fatima about. After a long meal filled with conversation about both of their lives, including what had tragically happened to London's parents and her beloved grandmother on graduation day, the girls took their coffee to go. Although London really missed Kenya and her best friend Amber, she had a feeling Fatima would stick by her side no matter what.

"So, girl, I see all these pictures of your family, including that fine-ass uncle of yours, but I don't see not one picture of you and your man. What's up with that? You don't strike me as the lesbo type, so spill. What's the deal with that?" Fatima was waiting for an answer as London sadly started to look down at the floor. "Wow, I'm sorry, girl, did I say something wrong?"

"No, not really. It's just that people always ask me that. My sister was the one born with all the style and flair. She has all the good looks and gets the guys. I guess I'm just used to blending in the background when it comes to me and Kenya."

"Oh hell naw! You must be high or something. Y'all look exactly alike. So how can you think that she's the shit and don't think you are?" Fatima damn near snatched her roommate in front of the door mirror leaning against the wall and pulled the rubber band out of London's hair. "You need to open those pretty eyes and see what everyone else sees. That flawless skin, a pretty smile, and this long-ass hair! Girl, most sisters would pay good dough for a pack of weave this long!"

London felt good for once about what she saw in the mirror thanks to Fatima. Starting now, she would try to have more confidence in herself. London knew that she needed to stand on her own without Kenya and be more assertive, and believing in herself would be the first step.

When they finished unpacking and talking, it was almost close to daybreak. The freshman orientation started at 9:30 a.m. sharp, so the two girls decided to get some much-needed shuteye. They both wanted to be on time so Fatima set the alarm. For a change, since Gran's death, London didn't have to be the mother hen.

Chapter Seven

Kenya

"Damn, I can't take this. I gotta get some darker blinds in this bitch!" Kenya, peeking out from underneath her pillow, started her day mad. Always having a major attitude, she had the nerve to be pissed at the sun for shining so brightly into her private domain. Lifting her head all the way up, she looked over at the clock, which read 12:15 p.m. Overjoyed that her sister was not there waking her up early as usual, she found one reason to at least crack half of a smile. Eyes still partially shut, Kenya made her way into the kitchen, sliding her bare feet across the floor. "I need a cold glass of juice, maybe then I can wake up."

Sitting down on the couch, leaning her head backward, as funny as it seemed Kenya thought that she could hear the sound of quiet circulating throughout the entire house. But she was alone and lonely in that big, empty house, bored to death, and the truth of the matter was she knew it wasn't going to get any better. All the frontin' she did on a regular basis about wanting nothing more than for people in general to just leave her the fuck alone was catching up to her. "I gotta shake this bullshit," Kenya hissed, listening to the eerie vibrations of her heart beating. Right then and there she decided it was most definitely time to get put on by her dude. Without any more hesitation or delays, she dialed Ty's phone, who picked up on the first ring.

"What up, doe Kenya?"

"You crazy, you."

"What's the deal with you?"

"Just chillin' that's all. I just woke my punk-ass up."

"Oh yeah?" Ty had just started blazing his second blunt of the day. "Man, I started to call you last night and see if you wanted to hang, but fuck all that!"

"Huh?" Kenya asked, confused.

"Shit, did you see that fucking 'nigga, I'm gonna kill your ass' death look your uncle gave me yesterday? I mean, I ain't no sucker or no shit like that with mines but, well, you feel me."

Knowing that Ty was indeed a sucker with his in every sense of the word, Kenya decided to not call him out on being scared shitless of her uncle because she needed him to do her a solid. "Come on, guy," she started to lie, gassing his ego up. "I know you ain't intimidated by his old ass! Everybody knows my uncle is past tense with that gangsta bullshit he be running!" Kenya was laying it on thick knowing that, truth be told, on any given day of the year, her uncle could beat the dog shit outta Ty with one hand tied behind his back. "But hey, forget about that old nigga. I need to talk to you about some other shit. Remember what we talked about the other night?" Kenya whispered like someone else was in the room eavesdropping on their private conversation.

"Come on, girl, we talk about a lot of shit, what's the dealio? Be more specific."

"Damn, nigga, you know what the fuck I'm talking about! That Heads Up shit!" Kenya yelled at the top of her lungs, rolling her eyes.

"Oh yeah, hell yeah!" Ty was truly excited at this point. He then bossed up, practically taking over the entire conversation like he was an expert in stripperology 101. "Okay, here's the deal. Amateur night is tonight about ten. If you do good up on that stage shaking that ass, my man Zack will get you all the way plugged in every night." His preaching continued. "Oh yeah, you should make sure your hair and nails are tight. Oh yeah, and make sure you shave under your arms. When I see hoes up there swing upside down on the pole with gorilla hair in them pits, a nigga get sick to his stomach." Ty was going on and on, making Kenya madder and madder.

"Hold the fuck up, Negro! You going too damn far with this bullshit you trying to kick! When the fuck have you ever known my shit not to be topnotch and on point, please believe?" Kenya was fed up with Ty's store-bought pimp impression. "Look just call me later!" she screamed out in total frustration, slamming the phone down in his ear.

As she sat there Kenya, now in total hustle mode, started to think about the half-ass naked outfits she had in the closet and a pair of spiked heels just right for driving the average man out his mind. In the zone, it was then that she decided to partake in her regular "breakfast of champions"—a big-ass blunt. Deeply inhaling, she turned the television on. Still on the video channel from the night before, she got her a quick head-banging routine together guaranteed to make some cash.

Nightfall took its sweet time arriving. It was 8:45 p.m. and Ty had just called saying he was on his way to pick her up. Not in the least bit nervous, Kenya excitedly got her small-sized duffel bag together with two "scandalous even in the nighttime" outfits she'd picked out, and a towel. Her face was beat, looking just right. She had just got finished applying M·A·C high-gloss lipstick and her lashes were long. *Damn, bitch, you the shit!* She snapped her fingers in front of the mirror.

Beep, beep, beep.

Kenya heard Ty pull up in front of her house and blow his horn. She quickly reached down, swooping up her designer bag, throwing the strap across her shoulder. Grabbing her keys and cell phone, she took a deep breath. After one last quick glance in the mirror, she was out the door, headed for her new future and hopefully the road to riches. Reaching for the doorknob, the house phone started to ring as Kenya turned back, securing the last deadbolt lock.

London

Exhausted and worn out, both London and Fatima had made their way through a long list of longwinded distinguished speakers, knowledgeable alumni and upper-classmen, teachers, and various presentations. Staying up the night before talking and unpacking was starting to take its toll on the weary freshmen.

"Girl, I can't wait to get back to that bed. I'm so tired I think I'm going to pass out right here on this ground!" London stretched as she yawned, fighting back the urge to go to sleep on one of the benches that lined the way back toward their dorm.

"I know how you feel." No sooner had Fatima barely gotten the last word out of her mouth than she was unexpectedly interrupted by a tall, handsome man with light brown eyes. He extended his arm, reaching out to shake each of the girls' hands as he confidently introduced himself.

"Well hello, ladies, how are you both doing?" He was so smooth with his tone and overall demeanor both girls could hardly move, let alone speak to respond to his question.

London was the first to regain her composure. "Oh fine, we were, uh, uh, uh . . ." She was stumbling with her words, struggling to get a clear thought, something that she almost never did.

By that time, Fatima, also dumbfounded, snapped out of her trance, coming to her girl's rescue. "Hell, we're both doing well. We just came from the freshmen orientation in the plaza."

"Yes, I know. I was just at the orientation myself. I saw both you ladies over there. I'm Sanford Kincade." His smile was ultra bright and his winter white teeth were perfectly lined. "Matter of fact, if I'm not mistaken, I think one of you young ladies and I will get to know each other very well over the coming semester." Neither girl had a clue as to what their handsome, unannounced stranger was talking about. Each one looked both puzzled and confused. Seeing them speechless, he could easily tell by their expressions they were feeling lost and out of sorts. "Oh, I'm sorry, ladies, let me start over again. I'm Professor Sanford Kincade. I'm on staff and teach Intro to Political Science here at the university."

Giggling like middle school girls on the playground instead of grown, mature women in college, London and Fatima recklessly fumbled retrieving their class schedules out of their folders, praying that they were the one blessed to have this God of a man for an instructor. As each visibly anxious student searched for that small piece of paper, Sanford Kincade, conniving in mindset, already knew the outcome. With ulterior motives in store, he'd checked it out prior to introducing himself, as he watched the two of them earlier.

London was the first to find her schedule. "Oh wow, I guess it's me." She almost felt ashamed for being the lucky one. Fatima, sad faced, was a little disappointed, but happy for her newfound friend nevertheless.

"Well then, Miss Roberts, I guess I will see you in class and, Miss James, see you around campus." As soon as he was out of ear range, both girls started screaming.

"Girl, he was so fine I could barely move." Fatima held her hand close to her chest.

"Yes, he was handsome," London agreed. "But, Fatima, that man is almost old enough to be our daddy."

"Yeah, girl, you right, I would call him daddy!" Both girls, behaving silly without a care in the world, giggled all the way back to the dorm.

London, after settling down, decided to try to call her sister again that night but still didn't get an answer. She also tried calling Kenya's cell phone, but her twin changed numbers like she changed her panties. The concerned twin was starting to worry and wanted nothing more than to call her uncle. She wanted to ask him to go by the house and at least check on Kenya, but she knew that wasn't gonna happen, especially considering what had jumped off the afternoon she'd left. Her uncle was still probably and rightfully pissed about that fool Ty keeping Kenya out all night and Kenya's nasty attitude and disposition to being chastised.

London then called Carmen, her sister's best friend, on her cell phone. Thankfully, she had Kenya's latest number and gave it to her. After the first ring the voicemail picked up. A long song filled with all types of curse words filled London's ears before she heard Kenya's voice. When the beep finally came, London spoke.

"Hey, Kenya, it's me. I tried calling you last night. I'm okay, I just wanted to know if all is well. I know it's been only two days, but you understand. Call me, all right? Don't forget. *Say U Promise!*" She hung up the phone and fell fast asleep. London had no idea that back at home in Detroit, her sister's long night was just beginning.

Tastey

Ty watched Kenya's full, plump breasts bounce up and down as she ran down the stairs. The way that her low-riding track suit fit her ass alone was enough to get him paid. Anticipating a quick come up, he started to daydream about all the money he could get from working Kenya. Greeting each other with a smile and a small kiss on the lips, both of them were anxious about the night and what it would hold. They both had a different agenda for what they felt was going to happen when they got to the club.

"Girl, you look hot! Good enough for a brotha to eat." Ty's dick started to get rock hard. He grabbed Kenya's hand and placed it on his manhood. "Feel what I got waiting for that ass when we get back from making that bread!"

Kenya gave him a fake smirk and told him, "Maybe later," keeping game on pause. She was trying to keep her mind clear, and his "always wanting to fuck and suck for free" butt wasn't helping her pay any bills around her way. Kenya was really straight starting not to feel ol' boy and his nickel-and-dime hustle ways, but she was smart enough to wait until she got her foot in the door of the Heads Up and when she did, he was so over.

Ty, feeling like he was a big shot, pulled up at the club. Trying hard to appear to be a boss, he got valet, trying keep the big fella image up. As they made their way up to the front door entrance there was a gang of trick-ass niggas waiting to give up their paychecks, bill money, or even the loot owed to the next man on a sack.

Hell, fuck going inside the club! Kenya saw how they were eyeballing her; and she could get most of their dough out their pockets by just looking at their grimy-asses. Nevertheless, Kenya was on a mission that was bigger than dudes standing on line waiting to be hand searched by security. Johnnie Roberts's daughter was about that life and getting that serious longevity loot. Winning the amateur contest was her only objective so she could secure herself a permanent position and start making revenue on a regular basis. Moving her curvaceous body through the crowd, she saw a pool of strange, desperate faces watching her like she was a precious shipment of gold. There were just as many hands brushing across her ass on the sly like they were getting away with something.

"Okay, how about this! The next nigga who puts his hands on me without paying is getting his shit split to the white meat!" Kenya made it clear for all possible offenders to hear. She wasn't bullshitting one bit and it showed all over her face. "I ain't into fucking charity and ain't shit for free this way! You touch you fucking pay, flat out, straight like that!"

"Hey, Zack." Ty proudly beamed, showing that stupid-ass gap in his dental. "This is my main girl, Kenya." He smiled, sticking his chest out with pride like he was her pimp or some shit like that.

In between the guys in the crowd having to be told what was really good and now Ty acting like he owned her and her hustle, she went ham. "Main girl?" Kenya finally had enough of his ass. "Nigga, what? Please don't coach mines. You got me all fucked up in the game. Fall back and don't play yourself!"

Zack couldn't help smiling as he watched her put Ty's perpetrating-ass in his place. Easing back, letting her do what she did, he thought, *She is much prettier than any of the girls working here and, damn, that ass is banging. Plus, with that spunk, she could double as security.* Zack had to laugh out loud about that shit. He hated to halt the debate, but Kenya had to be informed about the rules for the contest if she planned on participating. Plus Zack knew Ty needed to go in a corner somewhere, get several drinks, and try to recover and lick all of the open wounds that she'd left to his weak mack game.

"Hello, Kenya, I'm Zack. You can follow me up to the office so that I can explain a few things and check your ID out if that's okay with you."

Kenya smiled and turned around to follow, making sure to give Ty's wounded ego the sho'nuff side eye. As she observantly scanned around the club and checked out the atmosphere, she noticed even the ugliest girls on the guys' laps, grinding like there was no tomorrow. She thought, *Shit, I guess pussy don't have a face around this here motherfucker.*

When they got up the stairs and to the office Zack shut the steel door. Amazingly it was quiet as the library that London often would drag her to if she let her. "Okay, Miss Kenya, first things first, let me check out your ID." As Zack looked it over, he started questioning her on other club-related issues. He asked her just what made her want to dance and did she think she could do it. Kenya thought for a second and was going to try to say something sassy, but quickly changed her mind when she saw that he was trying to be sincere.

"Bills, just a lot of bills that I anticipate accumulating real soon. I don't want to fall behind or be late on any payments. That would mess with my credit rating and I ain't trying to do that." Kenya had learned all about finances from Gran and the importance of a high score.

Not expecting that answer in a million years from a female only seconds away from swinging naked on a pole, Zack was truly impressed with her response. *Finally a girl with a little bit of common sense; well, not that much. She should be in somebody's schoolhouse,* he thought, but who was he to judge? He was here to make money and capitalize off of her beauty, not be a life-changing coach. Zack took his time before spoke. "You right, Kenya, good credit is a must in the white man's world." Even though he ran a strip joint, he still hated to see young girls go down the wrong path and get turned out or, worse than that, strung the fuck out on drugs. But, hey, the ID said eighteen and that made her grown, so she was just that—grown. She was fair game. If he could profit off of her beautiful ass, why not, he thought. "Well, it's like this. You dance two songs when you go on stage, one fast and one slow. On the second song drop your top." Zack watched for any signs of weakness or apprehension, but none showed. "The guys will try to cop a free feel when they slip the money in your G-string. So as long as they don't get to outrageous with the shit, just try to be polite, make your money and move on. The fellas in the house know it's amateur night, so we always got one fool who gets extra and tries to push his hand. Don't worry about him; we got his ass covered. Be nice, but don't give the whole deal away for free. Remember, what one won't or can't do the next will. So don't listen to all that idle chitchat niggas wanna kick. Everything costs in this motherfucker, even conversation, so keep it moving!"

"Okay. Do I get to keep all of my tips?" Kenya eagerly awaited his answer, hoping it was yes.

"Yeah, tonight you do, but if you do good and you like it, you can get on the schedule. Then it's a house fee of fifty dollars a night, a fee for the DJ, and you should always tip Brother Rasul. He's the head of security. My man doesn't drink, curse, or mess around with any of the girls, which keeps him on top of thangs. He's one hard-ass Muslim brother. I think that's what makes him have such a low tolerance for men disrespecting our black queens, even if they choose to disrespect themselves up in here. That's why most niggas don't even try him. Shit, they'd be better off smacking Jesus off the cross than fucking with that guy. So, take care of him. Shiiit, even I tip Brother Ra! That being said you should be good to go."

Suddenly there was a knock at the door. "Enter!" Zack yelled out, looking over at the security camera while buzzing the door.

Walking through the door as if she owned the place was a woman with a long blond and red streaked weave.

It was untamed, reaching down to her ass, which was wide as hell, but she carried it well. She was at least forty or so in age, or so the wrinkles around her eyes revealed.

"Hey, baby. We got like eight girls in the dressing room for amateur night and the crowd is growing restless. So are you about ready to start the contest or what?" The older, fashionably dressed woman grinned while rubbing on Zack's balding head with her long multicolored painted fingernails.

"Yeah, in about ten minutes. This is the last girl for tonight. So if anyone else shows, tell them to come back next week. Besides, I think we have the winner right here." Zack winked his eye at the young future contestant.

"I see, I see. Hey, sweetheart, my name is Angela, but everyone around here calls me Old Skool. I'm sort of the house mother I guess."

"Hello, I'm Kenya Roberts, but you can call me . . ." She paused to think all of two seconds before she blurted out the name Tastey, since Ty had said she looked good enough to eat. "Yeah, call me Tastey."

"Okay, Miss Tastey, follow me."

When they reached the dressing room you could automatically tell the veterans from the rookies. While the vets were fixing their hair and stashing their loot, they still found time to mean mug all the fresh-faced, wide-eyed girls who were entering the contest hoping to win the prize money. After all, some of these green hoes had the potential to be their new competition, so there positively was no love lost. Of course, Kenya's thick model-type ass, when dressed and ready to compete, was getting a gang of major hate from both sides of the fence, new and old. Some of the girls couldn't even walk in heels let alone dance, while some of them needed to hit the gym at least five days a week. But even the ugliest females made a little bit of lunch money for the week in a dark, dimly lit strip club.

"Hey, girl, you ready? You about next." Old Skool was hyping Kenya up, whispering in her ear. "Girl, you got this shit. The prize money got your name on it. These other females are terrible!"

"Prize money?" Kenya was shocked hearing about that part of the contest for the first time. *Ty slick-ass ain't shit!* "How much is first place?"

"Two hundred bucks!"

"Oh yeah, you right, that two hundred dollars is mine. I'm about to wild the fuck out when it's my time to shine!" Kenya needed that cash like a baby needed his bottle.

A girl who the DJ said went by the name Raven was just making her way down off the stage. From where Kenya stood, she was her only real competition. The other girls in the contest were throwing shade on her also, so the two of them kinda stuck close by the other in case they might have to scrap. "Girl, them fools out there are on the nut. Watch yourself," a breathless Raven advised Kenya before she headed up.

"Okay, good lookin'." Kenya exchanged smiles with her, glancing over her shoulder, heading toward the small set of stairs.

"All right now, fellas, ballas, and any of y'all wannabe playas! This next girl has enough boom boom on deck to snap them zippers on sight!" The DJ was out his shit in the zone as he did his thang on the mic, making the energy level in the already-hot, humid club rise. "Take your hands out your pants and put them together for the one we affectionately call Tastey! Make her feel at home and make that shit rain Heads Up style!"

As Kenya entered the stage, you would have thought that she hit the winning homerun in game seven of the World Series. "Damn, girl, shake that shit," was all she kept hearing from the intoxicated patrons who were throwing currency her way. Kenya only saw dollar signs and didn't give a fuck what them fools was saying as long as that bread kept raining on the stage. Kenya, off deep into the loud sound of the speakers and the song she'd requested to be played, made eye contact with Ty just in time to see him abruptly rushed out the door by security. *Damn, I guess his "wannabe slick"and "work a bitch" knew it was over.* She giggled to herself as she moved like a seductive snake across the cash-covered stage.

The contest was soon over and, without a doubt, Kenya had won first place. With $200 plus another $150 in tips it was the best five minutes of her young life. She now had her foot in the door of Heads Up; hell, both feet, for that matter. And it was time for her to grind!

Chapter Eight

London

The first day of classes began and London was more than ready. She had one morning class and another in the evening starting at 6:30. This was a day that she'd been looking forward to her whole life. She was up, dressed, and out the door before Fatima had even turned over. She didn't have her first class until later. No sooner than London left did the phone start to ring repeatedly. The constant noise of the ringer woke a tired Fatima out of her coma-like sleep.

"Yeah, hello," Fatima's voice was groggy and she sounded completely out of it.

Kenya was hesitant about speaking up because she thought she had the wrong number.

"Hello," Fatima said again, this time with a slight attitude from being disturbed by the phone.

"Yeah, can I speak to Amia Roberts?" Kenya finally blurted out.

Fatima was thrown off for a second, when she remembered that London's real name was Amia. She sat up in the bed and wiped the sleep out of her eyes. "Sorry, she's not in. Whom should I tell her called?"

"This is her sister," Kenya spoke in a cold tone.

"Oh, Kenya! Hey, girl!" Fatima greeted her like they were old friends.

Kenya was kinda fucked up that this stranger knew who she was right off the bat. "Yeah, this is Kenya, and who are you?"

Fatima could tell by the tone in her voice that she was the twin who had got all the bad demons floating inside of her. She tried her best to be nice to her roomie's sister and not go all the way out on her for being rude and disrespectful so early in the damn morning. "Hey, I'm her roommate, Fatima James. Your sister told me all about you, besides, your picture is posted all around the room walls in here." Fatima was still trying to be polite, as hard as Kenya was making it.

"Okay then, bet, tell her I called. Peace." Kenya was still being somewhat a total bitch and it came across. With that exchange, she hung up on Fatima.

After finding out that her sister was off to her classes, Kenya decided to get herself some rest; after all, she had just made it home from the club and a long night of getting money.

London

The start of London's second class was full of anticipation. That was the class that Professor Kincade taught. As she entered the room she saw him standing behind his desk with papers in his hands. He looked so handsome. This was the first man she really ever had a crush on. London was always deep in her studies and had no time for the silly boys at her high school. Anyway, they were always interested in her sister, so her even caring about them was a waste of time.

Professor Kincade waited until everyone got seated and greeted all of his new freshman students. He then went in his briefcase and pulled out a huge stack of papers. "Miss Roberts, can you please come up here?"

London was stunned. What did he want? What would he say? When she reached his desk, she could smell the scent of cologne on his shirt as she walked up. "Yes, Professor Kincade?"

She was a nervous wreck and he could tell. Having what some would call classic good looks, he had this effect on most of the female students he'd come in contact with and some of the female professors.

"Yes, can you pass this course syllabus out for me?" With a smooth way about himself, he made sure to lock his eyes on London's, touching her hand as he handed her the papers. For an older man, he swore he had game. Known as a womanizer around campus, he wanted this young girl and was going to have her.

When class was over, he watched her youthful ass sway from side to side. His dick got hard just thinking about riding that untamed, tender cat. A true freak, he couldn't wait to get home so he could fuck his wife with London on his mind. This was his second marriage and even though his wife was only twenty-five, the professor had a taste for some younger pussy every now and then. And this was one of those times.

"Did you see that fine-ass Professor Kincade?" Fatima was just making it in from her own classes.

"Yeah, I not only saw him, he asked me to hand out some papers. I was scared as hell." London had chills as she told the story. "I wish I could be more like my sister. Kenya would have had him shaking in his boots."

Both girls exchanged stories of how their day went. Fatima, socially conscious, told her about some clubs that they could join. All the organizations were based on helping to try uplifting the black man and women as a whole.

"Wow, that sounds like where we need to be then." London was more than excited to attend the meeting. "When is it?"

"It's tomorrow evening at six o'clock at the student union." Fatima was overjoyed that London was interested and cared about helping her race just as she and her parents did.

"Trust me, I'm already there!" London reassured her.

The two roommates looked in their mini refrigerator and didn't see anything they wanted and agreed to go get some food across campus. London and Fatima put on their track pants and hoodies and jogged over to the cafeteria just before it was closing for the night.

"Dang, we just made it." London was out of breath as was Fatima.

Both girls picked out a few of the sandwiches that were on the counter and left. As they were heading back to their dorm room, London saw two students holding hands, walking, and wondered if she would ever have anyone to hold hands with in her life. She was eighteen years old and had never been kissed. She could vote and even go fight for her country, but hadn't found someone to love her. *Why can't I be more like Kenya?* she heartbreakingly thought.

When the two freshman students made it back to their dorm room, they decided to do a little studying and then hit the sack. Fatima and London couldn't wait to see what the meeting they would attend the next evening was going to be about. They talked about what to expect, until they both fell asleep.

Morning came soon enough and both girls took their turns at the showers and got dressed. London took her time picking out an outfit. She knew she would see Professor Kincade and she didn't want to look too corny. After going through almost all her clothes in the closet, she picked out a blue and black skirt with a black thin-material turtleneck and a cute pair of Prada mules that Kenya bought her for their birthday, so she knew they were fly as hell. London looked in the mirror and was satisfied. She was headed out the door when Fatima yelled out to her, "Hey, don't forget about six o'clock tonight!"

"I won't," London replied. "Six o'clock!"

London made it to her first class right on time. She tried to pay attention to the instructor, but found it hard to think about anything other than the next class awaiting her. Time was ticking by slowly, but finally past. *Thank God,* she thought. It was one o'clock and her first class was finally over.

London ate a late lunch and realized it would soon be time for the start of the next class. *I want to remember to check my teeth for any food before I go in there.* When 2:45 came, it was time. London made her way through the door and looked toward the front of the class. To her dismay, there was no sight of him yet.

"Hello, I'm Donyae." It was the guy who sat next to London at her earlier class. "We must have the same major." He was all in her space.

"Yeah, you might be right." London was having a hard time paying attention to him as he tried to kick game. He was trying his best to flirt with London, but her thoughts were on the professor and the smile that she couldn't seem to get out of her mind.

"Maybe we could study together sometime?" He tried to make eye contact with her, which was almost an impossible task since she was watching the classroom door like a hawk.

"Oh yeah, maybe," she finally stated nonchalantly, hoping he would give her some air.

Donyae was happy to get a maybe, so he sat down. Besides, the professor was coming.

"Good afternoon, everyone." He scanned the room until he saw London, making sure to acknowledge her presence. In class, they took notes on everything that they would be tested on that semester. By the time it was over, every student had a notebook full of information. "Well, that's it for today, have a nice evening." After that announcement, the room started to clear out.

"Hey, now, I was just wondering, can I walk you somewhere?" Donyae waited anxiously for her response, hoping that London would say yes.

"Well, umm . . ." Before London could complete her sentence, Professor Kincade interrupted the two.

"Excuse me, Miss Roberts, can I speak to you a moment?"

Donyae was disappointed that Professor Kincade had blown his rap to London. "Well, I'll see you later." He grinned at her as he left the room.

"Did I stop a future love connection from taking place?" Professor Kincade was smiling when he said it, but was really slightly jealous of the young boy's youth and the body that he once had when he was his age.

"Not really, I just met him today." London blushed at his assumption.

"Well, I was wondering, could we get a cup of coffee and discuss if you would like to be my class secretary?"

London was beaming with pride that he would even consider her for that seemingly important position. She had no idea that he'd made that title up at the last moment. He had to get a hold of that ass before Mr. Young and Smooth had a chance to. The professor was on a mission and didn't want to take any chances. Grabbing his briefcase they walked across the grass until they reached his car.

"Where are we going?" London felt strangely scared. Not really scared of him personally, but scared she would not know what to say to him in a one-on-one setting. London's heart was pounding. "The student union?"

"Oh no, I forgot the paperwork in my office. It's right at the edge of campus. Come on, jump in. I don't bite." Professor Kincade coaxed her inside his car.

After a short ride filled with jazz playing on the radio, he pulled up at an office building. He quickly ran in and returned with a look of total confusion on his face, giving London a sad expression. "I'm sorry, the office is such a mess that I couldn't find them and I didn't want to keep you out here waiting." The professor was definitely running his game. Real talk, he'd gotten just what he had come for and had it tucked discreetly in his pocket until the right time presented itself.

"Oh, that's okay. I have to go to a meeting in about an hour or so anyway." London was somewhat relieved because she was at a loss for words.

With the chances of his plan unraveling, he had to think quickly. "Hey, I promised you a cup of coffee. I know a place nearby." Turning right, then left, he pulled up to a little cafe before London had time to protest. They took a seat near the back area even though it wasn't that crowded inside. London wanted to sit on the front patio outside, but he claimed he was recovering from a cold. In reality, the wolf in man's clothing really had no desire to be in the front on display to the other patrons. He needed to be low-key; after all, he was a married man, and, besides, it would not fit into his cynical plan.

The teacher and young student continued to chat about this and that. Soon London checked her watch, and although she was having a good time, she revealed she would have to leave soon. It was already 5:15 and she didn't want to be late. Fatima would be waiting for her and she had no desire to let her new friend down. No man was worth losing a friend over; at least that's what Gran had taught her and Kenya. Sadly, she told the professor of her prearranged plans as she excused herself to go to the ladies' room.

Moments after she left out of sight, he reached in his pocket and pulled out a small vile: the same vile he'd gotten from his office earlier when they stopped. He put three small drops in her coffee and stirred it up, placing her spoon back in the same position. When the naïve teen returned and drank the rest, it seemed to be only minutes before she looked a little out of it.

"Wow, I feel kinda dizzy." London was starting to slur her words. She had never even tasted wine before so she had no idea about what she was starting to feel. The room was starting to spin and she felt confused and tired.

The professor sat back and watched London transform before his eyes. His dick started to get harder and harder as he thought about what was getting ready to take place. *It's show time.* For everything to go as planned, the scheming older man had to walk her to his vehicle before anyone else noticed her being tipsy and out of it.

The professor got her inside his car and locked the doors. As they drove down the road London was in somewhat of a trance as the road started to vibrate and her eyes rolled toward the rear of her head. Taking full advantage of the skirt she had on Professor Kincade roughly shoved his hand in between her legs after moving her panties to the side. London was soon totally passed out cold and couldn't feel the blunt force of his fingers pounding in and out of her virgin insides. The professor slowly licked his fingers, tasting her moist juices as he pulled them out of her.

My dick is so fucking hard I can't wait, he sinisterly thought. *This freshman is finer than all the ones in previous years!*

After a short drive they pulled up to his destination and London's unfortunate fate that was awaiting—the North End Motel.

Chapter Nine

London

It had been a little more than six hours since London had called Fatima to come and help her. In distress and disoriented, London woke up with all of her clothes torn off. There was blood on the sheets and every part of her body had been terribly violated. She needed a few stitches and the doctors at the hospital wanted her to call the authorities and report the sexual assault. London, embarrassed and ashamed, would have no part of the police. She didn't confide in anyone except Fatima the true identity of who she knew had drugged and ultimately violated her.

When London revealed to Fatima the rapist's name she was pissed all the way the fuck off. When she went to get London's class drop slip signed from the professor's bitch-ass, Fatima spit directly in his face, daring him to do or say something. Knowing he'd get undoubtedly fired or, worse than that, arrested and thrown in jail if the news of his dirty deed surfaced for all to know, he remained silent. He knew at this point, with Fatima's saliva dripping down his face, it was true; he couldn't say or do anything for fear of any police involvement. The professor, usually in total control of his antics, didn't know how he'd let shit get so out of control this time. Lowering his head in shame, he just signed the withdraw slip and wiped his face off with a napkin.

London, after a short time recuperating, made her way to the rest of her classes that semester, and, although she was mentally stressed, maintained fairly good grades all things considered. Wanting to forget the entire tragic event, she finally made it to a few of those socially conscious meetings that she'd missed that night six months ago.

When Thanksgiving came, as well as Christmas, London had gone home with Fatima. It was nice being around a family, a real family, with people who loved each other. Fatima's family were Muslim and didn't celebrate Christmas but they still got together for a big dinner so they could all bond and catch one another up on their current activities. London, engulfed in the atmosphere of family, could tell where Fatima got her caring ways.

Besides a few calls here and there, it was like she had cut herself off entirely from her own small-sized family. Her uncle had his woman still send her money every now and then when she could, even though her man had gotten knocked again and was serving time. This bid unfortunately was for more than just a few months. He was doing a few years on a probation violation so any direct contact he had with London was limited to none.

It would soon be spring break and London would be going home for the first time since school had begun the previous year. Although she enjoyed college life despite what had happened between her and the professor, she did miss her twin sister Kenya. Sure they talked on the phone sometimes, but nothing could take the place of seeing her twin face to face. She needed to see her other half and make sure she was safe and sound.

Kenya

Kenya was doing it big at Heads Up. Ever since her first night of slinging that ass, she was getting more money than any other female in the spot. She was a topnotch dancer at the club and had multitudes of regulars who'd wait to give their money to her and only her. A lot of the other girls were mad jealous of her pole and twerking skills, but Kenya didn't give a shit. She was there to make cash, not friends. Only her girl Raven was rolling with her in that motherfucker. The two of them were tight and got paid no matter what.

"Hey, girl, you making that money tonight!" Old Skool was sitting at the bar with Kenya, nursing a drink.

"Yeah, and you know it. I gotta get some new shit in my crib, maybe some heavy-duty steel doors or something like that." Kenya was being careful and big on security. She knew that crackheads back in the hood knew that she was getting that dough.

Zack walked over to his two favorite ladies in the club and kissed Old Skool on the cheek. "What you two over here scheming on?" Zack smiled as he attentively watched Raven up on the stage under the lights, wowing the crowd.

"Well apparently Miss Tastey here needs to step up her paper game." Old Skool put Kenya's business out in the street.

"Oh yeah, okay, what's the problem, Tastey, what you need?" He focused his attention back to them.

"Well, I think I need to switch up a little bit. I don't want to get played out." Caught up in the club life of mutual respect for a hardworking dancers' world, she walked over to the stage and gave her girl some love. "Damn, why don't you ho-ass niggas get ya panties out ya ass and tip a bitch?" She was going off on everyone within ear range who was gawking at Raven instead of throwing dollars. "What's the problem? Did y'all losers leave your purses in the fucking car?"

The DJ even had to laugh at that shit as Zack, Old Skool, and Brother Rasul, who just walked up, stood by, watching Kenya go hard.

"Maybe we should think about putting Tastey on," Zack pondered as Brother Rasul listened, not saying a word. "Kenya's kinda green, but it might work if we work it right."

Having a special place in his heart for the way she would carry herself nightly if she felt she was being disrespected, Brother Rasul always looked out for Kenya since day one. Kenya was a true hustler, not like most of the dick handlers in the club he'd watch sell their bodies for an extra dollar or two. The young girl was all about the money and the business that came with it. Brother Rasul shook his head and walked away, not wanting any part of what Zack was about to do. Zack was his boy and all, but he hated the way he took advantage of some of the girls.

Zack decided he would speak to her next week about what he and Old Skool had planned. Kenya was going to take a few days off to take care of some personal matters she claimed to have pending. He had no idea whatsoever that Kenya had a sister, let alone a twin. No one she worked with or for in the club knew about London. That was her life outside the strip club. They were two different worlds and Kenya planned to keep it that way for as long as possible.

After her long double shift had ended, it was finally time to get off of work. Kenya, worn out, but elated, couldn't wait to see her sister.

Reunion

Damn, I gotta hurry the fuck up and get all this stuff put away. There ain't no way in hell I can have this place on the nut when London gets home. She might bug out and kill a bitch if she saw the mess that been piling in this house since she left. Kenya had taken time off from the club to initially clean the house and spend some quality time with her sister. London was coming home for spring break and the two hadn't seen each other in months.

After hours of washing dishes and cleaning top to bottom, Kenya was tired as shit. No sooner than the last dish was put away did she hear London's key turn at the door.

"Kenya!" London yelled as she made her way inside the front hallway.

Kenya jumped from around the doorway and started smiling. "Girl, you know Gran told your butt not to yell in this house with your rude-ass!"

They both ran to each other and hugged for what seemed like forever. Tears were flowing from both twins' eyes. "I missed you so much," they both said at the same time. "Me too." Once again they said it together. It was like they were reading from a script or something. It was one of the things twins were famous for and these two were no different.

When they finally got all of London's bags in the house, they got a good look at one another and noticed some changes. Kenya didn't have on her makeup and was dressed in sweats. Her nails were still manicured perfectly, but she just seemed so much more slowly paced than London had remembered. Being on display at the club ten hours a day made Kenya just want to relax more at home and take life easy. She learned how to love to be plain ol' Kenya instead of flashy, flamboyant Tastey: queen of Heads Up.

London, on the other hand, was different as well. There were a lot of huge visible changes. She had started wearing her shoulder-length hair down and wore clothes that were more suited for a girl her own age than someone's grandmother. London wasn't always outspoken, but now she was sure of herself and held her head up when she would speak. She was even downright loud as hell if need be to get her point across. Between Fatima's coaching, her club and organization meetings, and that creep foul bullshit that Professor Kincade did, she'd become a much stronger individual. London was a new person with a new attitude, and it showed.

"Okay, now tell me everything that has been happening around since I left. How are Carmen and Allan? Where is that no-good Ty? Tell me everything!" London was excited to be home as she plopped down on the couch, kicking her shoes off.

Kenya was almost knocked off her feet by her sister's newfound bubbly personality. "Damn, bitch, slow your roll!" She was laughing like crazy by this time and so was London. It was like old times when they were kids, but the tables had turned. The difference was now London was holding court and Kenya was sitting back enjoying the show.

London told her sister all about Fatima and how she always had her back at school, how well her family had treated her on the holidays, and how she even had called Fatima's mother "Mama James."

Initially Kenya was slightly jealous hearing about Fatima, but she had her own little family at the club so she understood where her twin was coming from. Her, Raven, Zack, Old Skool, and Brother Rasul were just like family at Heads Up. Shit, Old Skool had even cooked a gigantic Thanksgiving dinner for them and all the dancers who didn't have or were shunned from their biological family. Even if they did eat it at the club at the same tables they'd shake their naked asses on, it was still all good. They were together and to Kenya that meant something.

London begged Kenya to promise not to get upset when she confessed to her about the brutal rape and the physical and mental condition it had left her in. By the time London bravely finished the story, all hell was about to break loose. She had to beg her sister to slow the fuck down. Kenya was screaming about calling someone named Brother Rasul to kill Professor Kincade and his whole generation by nightfall or as long as it took to drive back up to the university. After nearly fifteen minutes of trying to calm her twin down, London finally got a chance to ask her sister one question, which was, "Who in the heck is Brother Rasul?"

That opened the door for Kenya to tell her about her job and her new friends. Kenya explained to her sister how her new friends were a little different than a traditional family, but they all cared about each other. She explained to her how Brother Rasul taught her about Islam and how she told him about what the Bible meant to her.

London, who learned about the Islamic faith from Fatima, listened with an open mind as Kenya went on to tell her how Zack taught both her and Raven about accounting, so when they started their own business, no one could cheat them. London also soon found out that Kenya was even godmother to Raven's infant son, Jaylin. Kenya said she loved Jaylin just like he was her very own flesh and blood. She wanted the very best for him and even paid for his daycare when Raven would be short.

Though London might not have agreed with her sister's choice of work to make a living, she was glad that she had love in her heart for someone other than herself. London was happy to learn her twin had thankfully got rid of that self-serving Ty and even happier to learn that Carmen and Allan had gotten a place together on the east side of Detroit and were in school trying to get degrees.

"Okay, what about Amber? Where is she? Have you seen her lately?" London was worried about her best friend. "Last time I called her number a recording came on saying it was disconnected. I called her job and they told me she got fired."

Kenya hated to tell her what she really knew about Amber, so instead she put on her shoes and had London to walk to the store with her. When they reached Linwood Avenue and turned the corner, London glanced around, and surveyed the neighborhood. She could tell that much had not changed.

"Same blight, same drunks, same crackheads. We need to do something to help our people," she sadly remarked.

No sooner than those words came out of her mouth did they run into what Kenya didn't want to say: it was Amber. She looked torn the fuck up! Her hair was nappy and she smelled just like, like . . . fuck it, you know! The bitch was foul, a real shit bag! Kenya was overwhelmed and nauseated by the awful stench that surrounded Amber's every step. Her eyes watered from the repulsive aroma that filled the air and she quickly turned away so she wouldn't pass out from having to hold her breath.

"Oh my God! What happened, Amber? What happened?" London cringed at the sight of her friend and started to cry.

Kenya couldn't do anything but stand mute and let her sister get that shit out. When she first saw Amber tricking in the alley, she was shocked too. That pipe had taken complete control over Amber's young life and was now running things.

Amber glanced over at London and then focused her eyes toward the litter-filled ground. All she could do was be ashamed. She kicked her dingy and battered shoes against the curb as she tried explaining her new life to London. "After you left, I started hanging with Chuck and 'em. One night we was drinking and I decided to just try a little. I swear I can stop, girl!" Of course, Amber was lying to London and herself; she was too far gone to stop just like that.

"Well, okay then, walk back to the house with us!" London pleaded repeatedly. "Let me get you some help!" She wanted to put her arms around her best friend and reassure her that everything would be all right, but between the terrible smell and the open sores on Amber's face, London couldn't bring herself to do it. Amber was too far gone on that glass pipe to be turned around, at least not today. She and the drug were in a committed monogamous relationship, deeper than any marriage.

"I'll be around there later, I promise." Amber licked her dry, cracked lips as she tried to fix her hair. At this point she was telling London anything that popped into her mind because that ten dollars she had just sucked dick for in the vacant house was calling her to get a rock. Amber looked at London one last time, embarrassed, as she started to cry, and ran off down the street to get high.

"Kenya, I can't believe that mess. Why didn't you warn me?"

"Girl, what you want me to say?" Kenya was giving her sister a look that would kill. "That your friend is a li'l crack ho? Is that what you wanted to hear?"

London openly sobbed, trying to get some answers. "Why didn't you try to help her Kenya? Huh? Why?"

"Now wait! Hold the fuck up, don't get it twisted. That's your girl, not mine! I don't have time to be chasing a head all around town! Plus, oh yeah, I heard what you said, and don't be having her all up in my fucking house!"

"Kenya, how can you say that? She needs help. And don't forget, it's half my house too!" she replied, feisty.

"Well, okay then, when we get home, take a good look around, London. Everything that's worth stealing in that son of a bitch is mine, so fuck the dumb shit and recognize! That crack ho ain't never stepping foot in that motherfucker, so you can take that shit how you want it, half yours or not!"

***

Over the next few days that followed the twin's reunion, they realized just how much the two had changed. London had stepped her game up and now was a vocal leader around campus. She was about to branch out and help start an organization that would target the problems of black youths in school who had come from drug-addicted households. Seeing people being messed up by drugs, and now Amber, was eating away at her. Whether or not Kenya wanted to admit it, drugs had killed both their parents, leaving them orphans.

"After I saw Amber the other day, I made up my mind that it was time. I've put this off long enough. It needs to stop." London was up on her soapbox again as Kenya tried her best to ignore her.

"Dang, girl, stop all that loud talking!" Kenya was tired of her sister being all caught up in her feelings. "I know what you're saying and all and I'm proud of you for real, but damn why you gotta be so high-pitched and shit? Shut the fuck up, damn!"

"I'm sorry, I just can't understand what made Amber go that way. Your boy Allan grew up with his mother using drugs and made the decision to not follow in her footsteps."

"Well, that's life in the big city, London." Kenya walked to the kitchen and looked in the empty fridge. "Let's go out to breakfast."

"All right, let's go," London easily agreed, and thought that she would try to press her luck. "Why don't we go see if Amber wants to go? Maybe we could talk to her."

"Listen here, girl, we fam and all, but you bugging if think her ruthless behind is rolling out with me! She smells like something crawled up in her ass and died! Come on now, London, be for real! Do you really think I'm going out like that?" Kenya laughed at her sister. "Girl, ain't no stopping a head!"

London knew her twin was right, only on the fact that Amber would feel out of place. "Well, all right then, I'm ready." London knew better than to try to change her sister's mind.

The girls jumped in Kenya's car and rode about ten minutes before they reached the Black Bottom Cafe. It served the best breakfast around the D and at night it turned into a showcase where folks could show off their poetry skills. After a short wait to get a table, the girls were seated near the back in a booth. They checked out the menu as the waitress brought London the cup of coffee that she ordered as soon as they sat down.

Kenya was the first to really bring up their beloved Gran. They both seemed to avoid any real deep conversations about her so, they wouldn't cry. "I see Gran still got that ass drinking coffee." Kenya was shaking her head, placing the menu on the table.

London grinned, shrugging her shoulders. "Yeah, I drink it like water."

"I'm glad you came home, London. I need to talk to you about a few things. I have felt this way for a couple of months, but didn't know how to bring it up."

"What is it? We're sisters, we shouldn't keep secrets." London put her cup down and waited for her twin to speak.

"Well . . ." Kenya looked in her sister's eyes. "I think we should try to sell the house."

"What house? Gran's house? Are you crazy?"

"You mean our house, London. Gran is gone!" Kenya blurted out with no remorse for her sister's feelings. "It's ours, London, you and me."

"I know she's gone, but damn, she worked hard to keep that house!" London was now slightly raising her voice.

"I know, but it's so big!" Kenya pouted as she folded her arms and continued, "Big and lonely. You're at school.

You're gone, living your life. I gotta keep that bitch clean. I'm the one who has to keep the snow shoveled, the grass cut, and leaves raked. Pay all the utilities."

"Look, I understand what you're saying, but that's our childhood in that house," London insisted, hoping to change her twin's mind.

Kenya was tired of all that back-and-forth bullshit. She was the only one holding that house down. She was going to come at London with the only thing that she seemed to now understand and embrace: struggle.

"First of all, London, the taxes and the water bill are due this month. You got half? Next, the homeowners insurance; once again, do you got half on that? And then, sorry, I had almost forgotten about the heating and light bill that are being shut off. Let me get out a pencil and paper and total your part." Kenya was pissed by that point and was now raising her voice.

London was totally thrown off by her sister's callous outbreak. She totally was speechless.

Kenya didn't let up. "You see the neighborhood, London. You see how it's changing. Even your own girl, Amber, is setting people up. Go ask Old Mr. Phelps. He'll tell you! Shiiit. How you gonna carry it, London? Stop chasing a dead dream. Our hood is off the fuckin' hook. These fools out here ain't playing no more little kiddie games! They playing hardball!"

London knew her twin was telling the truth about the state of the neighborhood, and even Amber; although, she still knew that Gran wouldn't want the house sold to strangers. "You know I need all my money to pay for extra school expenses next year. Kenya, I can't spend it!"

"Oh, I get it, so you think it's all right for me to spend all of my damn money? Well news flash: the money Gran left me is gone. And now I gotta get mines how I live. I hustle, London. I live day by day, no doubt. Some nights,

I'm scared to come home to my own house because of the damn crime, so fuck what you talking about."

London got her thoughts together and finally spoke. "Listen, Kenya, just let me think about it. Let's just eat our breakfast and talk more about it at home."

"I'm sorry that I threw you off your square, but I don't know what else to do. You know I got love for you." Kenya and London smiled at one another and decided to change the subject. That one had run its course for the moment.

When the waitress brought the bill to the table both girls reached for it at the same time. "Let me get that. I know how you 'need' your money." Kenya laughed as she excused herself to go to the bathroom.

London watched her sister walk through the restaurant like she owned the place. *Some things never change!* London thought.

"Hey, Tastey, I missed you last night, with your fine self. You know how I get when I can't get a 'taste'!" A strange guy appeared at the table. The man was leaning all in London's inner space. "Here, baby, let me take care of your bill." He pulled out a wad of cash and peeled off three twenty dollar bills. "I'll see you this weekend, baby." He made sure to touch her hand when he put the cash on the table. London had a flashback of Professor Kincade and was in a frozen trance. He then smiled and went back to the other side of the room to sit with his friends, who were all staring.

Kenya returned to the table, putting lotion on her hands. She saw the money on the table and shook her head at London. "Listen, Ms. Goody-Goody, I told you I had it," she said, and slid the loot back over to her.

"I didn't pay for it, Tastey!" London rolled her eyes. Kenya immediately looked puzzled when she heard her sister call her by her stage name. "Some guy over there thought I was you, or should I say 'Tastey,' and paid for it." London pointed toward the group of desperate-looking men.

Kenya just shrugged her shoulders and nodded her head at them. "It's all part of the game! Life in the hood! Some of us can't escape!"

It was then that London decided to agree to put the house up for sale. She didn't want her sister to have to live right in the mix. Even as soft as everyone thought she was, she knew that you didn't shit where you slept.

Chapter Ten

Tastey

It had been a little over a month since the girls parted ways. They decided that over the summer they would indeed sell the house, and started to pack up most the stuff they wanted to keep. London would be home from school then and would have time to spare. Kenya was spending a lot of time at work. Being both Kenya at home and Tastey at work would sometimes get confusing. Kenya was now starting to turn into her stage name even at home. She was living and breathing the club and all the club life had to offer. It seemed like her government name was starting to become almost nonexistent.

"Hey, Zack, what's good?" Tastey was in great spirits and it showed.

"You, baby, you know that," he replied with his normal charm and swag.

"Look, I need to talk to you later." Tastey had a game plan in mind. "But, I gotta make this paper right now. One of my regular customers just came in and I don't want to keep his trick-ass waiting."

"Do you, baby girl. I'll be posted here all night." He loved to see her in action, getting that dough. Tastey made his club outshine all the others in the city. Zack was glad that she wanted to talk to him. All about a scheme, he also had a few things to discuss with her as well. He wanted to first run his thoughts by Old Skool and see what she thought he should do. A friend and confidante to all the dancers, she would know the right way to come at Tastey concerning his proposition. He knew that the young girl was a little streetwise, but was she street ready?

"Hey, darling, you needed me?" Old Skool came out of the dressing room as soon as she got the message that Zack wanted to speak with her.

"Yeah, I need to see what you think about that shit we talked about last month." Zack leaned back on the barstool.

"What shit? You know a bitch catching years!" Both her and Zack laughed she looked deeply in his eyes. They went back, way back, when Old Skool was considered "young game."

"I'm talking about that traveling thang, remember?"

"Oh yeah, that. I'm with that! I think Tastey would be able to pull the shit off. Matter of fact she's perfect. Raven is still a little green. Plus, she has a son and might not be able to roll that easy." Old Skool always thought ahead when planning anything.

"Well, I'm trying to figure out how to break on her without scaring her or running her out the club, you dig? She's my best moneymaker in here. Tastey makes all the other girls hustle more." Zack was in full scheme mode at this point.

"Yeah, you right, but I think she's trying to save money to get her an apartment anyhow. I think the crib where she lives at now is going to be sold soon. I overheard her and Raven talking."

Not only didn't Old Skool or Zack know that she had a twin sister, they had no idea she owned a house as well. They thought she was just another dancer renting a spot. They were used to all young girls who danced having nothing, not a pot to piss in nor a window to throw it out of. Tastey was different and Zack thought back to the day they first met. That's why he had to come at her just right to avoid her possibly going ham.

"You know what? I think I'm just gonna be real and take my chances. The game is served cold, like a bowl of ice cream, and I'm gonna give it to her just like that." Zack was on the money trail. His last hook up had been fucking up on the count and that just wouldn't do in his shady world.

Old Skool listened and was in total agreement with Zack. She watched Tastey from across the room while she was giving one of her regulars a lap dance. "She has game, I'll give her that much."

Game Face On!

"Damn, baby, you like that? Tell me you like how all this ass feels on your dick." Tastey was spitting game on Shawn. He was one of her regulars. "Oh, daddy, your dick is so hard. Is all that for me?" Grinning all in his face, the young temptress was careful to keep her eyes glued on him, knowing eye contact would keep him hypnotized. His manhood was rock hard so Tastey knew to ease up on the grinding. She didn't want him to bust a nut on himself. Well, not at least 'til she got four or five dances from him. At twenty dollars a pop that would be at least a hundred. By the time the fifth song was beginning, Ms. Tastey decided to let loose on him. She knew he was about at his spending limit and wanted to make sure that he was satisfied with the dance. She never wanted to make a customer of hers have to get another girl for a good time. "Please, let me turn around and ride you, daddy!" She was licking her lips. "I want you to watch me cum on that big black dick!"

Shawn was all in as he grabbed a hold of Tastey's waist. "Yeah, that's it, make daddy cum!" was all he could get out his mouth before Tastey filled his face with her breasts. She was moving back and forth and talking cash shit in his ear.

Brother Rasul was keeping a watchful eye, just in case she or any of the other girls needed him. Some of the dudes would sometimes get too excited and take the fantasy a little too far. That's when he would step in and try to damn near snap their necks. After a few more seconds, the song was over and Shawn had a huge smile on his face. He finished his drink and told Tastey that he would see her later on in the week. She really liked Shawn and secretly wished that it was her who was on the picture in his wallet, the one with his wife and baby. As she was trying to make it back into the dressing room to freshen up and change her outfit, a familiar hand reached from nowhere, grabbing out for her arm.

"Damn, motherfucker, what the fuck . . . ?" Before she could finish her sentence she realized that it was Ty. She hadn't really spoken to him since the night she started working at the club. He'd called, leaving a few threatening messages about her owing him for putting her on, but that didn't stop her from getting her money.

"Oh, I guess you just said fuck me and shit. It's like that? You dirty, rotten bitch!" Ty was drunk and slurring his words. "I'm the one who put your cum-catchin'-ass on in this motherfucker. You owe me. Why don't you come over here and give a nigga some of that famous head I've been missing out on?"

"Oh, you trying it! Listen, Ty, I don't owe you jack shit. You got me all the way twisted in this piece!" Tastey was pissed and aggravated as she put him in his place. "And don't come all up in my job trying to front!"

"Oh, wow it's like that? You a beast now, right?" He was on the nut and about to try to cuff her up by her throat, when out of nowhere a huge arm wrapped around his neck. Brother Rasul was choking the dog shit out of Ty as he struggled unsuccessfully to breathe. He was turning beet red and tears were flowing out both eyes. Zack, seeing the commotion, came running over just as Ty was getting skull drug out the door. "I was just . . ."

Ty couldn't get his explanation out good before Zack also started in on him. "Let me show you how real D-town ballers ball!" Zack reached under his shirt and pulled out a shiny black nine. He put one up top and put the gun in Ty's mouth. "Pay attention, Tastey or Kenya or whatever you choose to call her is family up here, all right! If you ever fucking choose to disturb her well-being again, I'll blow your dental out the back of your neck! Now get the fuck out my club before you get me all the way off my square. That's my word! We clear?"

Zack stuffed his gun back in his rear waistband and left Brother Rasul and the rest of the bouncers to do their thang. Tastey was feeling somewhat bad for Ty, but she felt strangely loved by Zack and the rest of her club family and felt a sense of loyalty to them for coming to her aid.

Old Skool, wanting to put her two cents in the mix, came in the dressing room and wanted to know if she was okay. "Hey, girl. You good or what?" She rubbed sympathetically on the young girl's back.

"Yeah, I just hate when someone tries to put a bitch's business all up in the street. It's all good though. I ain't tripping on it though."

"That's good. Don't let these fools front on you." Old Skool made her feel much better. "When you get dressed Zack wants to talk to you." Tastey gave her a worried look, hoping her job wasn't in jeopardy. "Girl, don't worry. He ain't bugging about that bullshit. He said you wanted to talk to him about some stuff you had on your mind."

"Oh yeah, damn, I did. I almost forgot!" Tastey was relieved. She didn't want to lose her job. She needed the money and, besides, she had no other friends except her girl Raven and the rest of the club family. Emotionally drained from dealing with Ty's over-the-top antics, she decided to be done for the night. She pulled her hair up in a ponytail and put on a track suit and her sneakers. She was getting herself prepared to meet with Zack.

Tastey made her way into Zack's office and took a seat on the couch. He was on his cell phone, talking a lot of shit as always. After a short while of listening to him boast about this, that, and the third, she got up and started to look at all of the different framed pictures he had on the office wall. There were a few of girls and some of cars, but most of them were nightclub shots from way back when. Judging from some of the outfits he and others had on, he must have been collecting them for a long time. In some of them, Zack's pimped-out-ass was even sporting a Jheri curl and bell-bottoms. As she walked along the wall, one picture shockingly jumped out at her. Tastey moved in extra close to get a better look, thinking her eyes might've been playing tricks on her. "Oh fuck naw, oh shit!" Her sudden outburst caused Zack to glance over at her and start to wrap up his conversation.

"What's up, baby girl? Sorry about that. You know how I am when I get to runnin' my mouth. I damn near forgot you were here you were so quiet." He was making his way toward her as he was talking.

Tastey made sure to move away from that particular picture so he wouldn't ask her any questions about her reaction to it. "Don't worry. I kept myself busy looking at all your pictures, especially the ones where you're busting that curl!" Kenya was laughing at Zack, trying to play off a bad feeling that was stirring inside the pit of her stomach.

Playing the role, he started acting like he was fixing his curl in the mirror. "You don't know nothing about this! I was Grand Daddy Caddy, Macaroni Tony!" Zack teased before getting down to the reason for their meeting.

After they sat down and got themselves together it was time to get to it. Zack thought it would be better to let Tastey start and get whatever it was that she wanted to say out in the open before he broke on her with his game plan.

"Okay, this is what I was thinking." She adjusted her body in the chair, praying his response would be positive. "What if we had feature dancers and showcases every week here? You know, some shit where the top moneymakers got put on full blast? I was talking to Old Skool and she told me she used to be a feature dancer at different spots around the city." Tastey took a break in the presentation she was making, to try to peep Zack and see if he was buying into her new hustle.

"That's what's up! I'm glad to see you're thinking of more ways to make the club and yourself extra revenue." Zack had to make sure to give Old Skool some extra cash and some of his dick that she always craved. She had perfectly laid the groundwork out for his plan and he was overjoyed. This was just what he needed to hear. Zack could manipulate Kenya into thinking that it was her idea and he came up with his part of it at the tail end, spur of the moment. "I think we can do that and even a little bit more."

Zack told her to get relaxed and pay attention to what he was about to say next. This was going to be the part of the plan that would make or break the whole deal. "All right, Tastey, here's the real thing that I'm talking about. I got a gravy-ass hookup with a couple of cats out West in L.A. and down in Texas. And we got sorta what you would call a partnership. You see, I got my hands on a lot of, should we say, product, and they're interested in helping me get rid of it." He was rubbing his hands together as he spoke, hoping to lure Kenya on his team. "First, we can do some smaller things in Ohio and other places closer to home, then move up to a bigger scale."

"Are you talking about moving cocaine, raw, or trees?" Kenya was attentively sitting straight up in her seat, taking in all her boss had to say.

"Hell naw! Now just what the fuck you know about all that?" Zack was more than amazed that she had come on him just like that, flat out with it. He was both shocked and relieved all at the same time. The expression on his face told it all.

Tastey could see that he was staring at her strange, so she took over the conversation. "Come on, Zack, you act like I don't be around people. You must think I'm not from the hood. Who the fuck ain't got a head in their family? And, shit, weed is the third creation. Everybody knows God made the heavens, the earth, and then the 'trees.'" Tastey held her hands open and looked toward the sky like she was smiling up at the Almighty Himself.

"Girl, you know you a fool!" It was then that Zack knew that his plan would work out perfectly. The scheming pair talked for close to a hour before Brother Rasul came to the door informing him that a guy was out front looking for him needing a face to face. He was claiming his business was very important and extremely personal, meaning that what he had to say was for Zack's ears only.

"Okay, partner, let me go up front and see what all this is about and I'll talk to you tomorrow, cool?" Zack reached over and grabbed Tastey's hand, shaking it, signifying they had a deal. "Be easy, baby girl, and clear your mind, you about to make some major paper."

As Zack and Tastey left out his office, he saw Old Skool sitting at the end of the bar and blew her a kiss as he stroked his dick. She knew that she would get paid tonight in more ways than one. Old Skool then told Tastey to have a good night as one of Brother Rasul's team walked her out to her car. Seeing something stuck underneath her windshield wiper blade, she took the half-folded paper out. Quickly realizing Ty had left the note, Kenya angrily balled it up and threw it out the window without so much as reading one single solitary word. *Fuck him and all that drama he be bringing with him!* As she pulled out the parking lot still thinking about the picture she'd seen on Zack's office wall, she drove home for the night.

Zack

"Young Foy, my nigga. Man, when did you come home? We missed you in the D." Zack gave his man a play and a short hug. "You did a real little bid this time around didn't you? Do them crackers up north know they done let a straight-up fool loose?" Zack laughed so loudly that some of the girls were alarmed thinking it was more trouble like what had jumped off earlier.

Young Foy was tall and had the build of most career inmates. With a hood mentality, he was a straight-up troublemaker, no doubt. If anything was being sold on the far west side of town he had a piece of the action, even if he had to strong-arm his way on the ticket. The seasoned criminal's temper was on a hairline trigger much like Kenya's. He would fly hot on that ass at the drop of a dime before you knew it. However, being in and out of prison never seemed to stop him from having his ear to the streets. Young Foy, although 100 percent thug, was always spitting rhymes and singing. He needed to get into show business and stop running in the streets before he got killed like most of the dudes he'd come up with. All he needed was a chance and someone to bankroll his dream.

"Hey, guy, I wanted to stop by and check on you. See what you had popping for a brother. You know a nigga fresh out and trying to come back up." Young Foy was running his game down. Playas in the hood knew he was a man of his word when it came to getting that money. "Let a nigga get some work! You know I straight need it!"

"I tell you what." Zack's mind was beginning to work overtime; besides, he knew when it came to Young Foy he'd have to cut him in or cut it out all together. "Stop by in the next few days and I can most def put you on. In the meantime, welcome home!" Zack dug in his pockets, respectfully pulling out two hundred-dollar bills, giving them to Young Foy.

"All right bet, bet, good lookin'." Young Foy then paused remembering the other reason he'd made a trip to see Zack as soon as he touched down. "Damn, dawg. It almost slipped my mind your boy Stone was locked up with me. He wanted me to make sure to come by and tell you that he needs you to come see him and shit as soon as possible."

"Yo, why didn't he just call the phone or drop a nigga a few lines? Do he need some dough or something?" Zack quizzed.

"Come on, killer, what I look like, Ms. Cleo?" Young Foy saw one of Zack's phat-ass freaks walk by and that was all she wrote for their conversation. He was on ho patrol. "Man, I'll holler. Just go get with dude! He acted like it was urgent." And with those words he was out.

Old Skool came over to Zack and put her arms around him. She couldn't wait to get to her house and get her hands on Zack's dick. "Hey, it's almost three, let's have Brother Rasul shut it down."

Zack agreed, kissing her on the lips. "Yeah, okay. Let's be out. After all, I owe your ass a little something-something and you know I hate owing a nigga." Old Skool gave him a yard of tongue, while he ran his hand across her thirty-six DDs. "We'll see you in the morning." Zack patted Brother Rasul on the back as they left for the night. He trusted him with his club and his life.

Chapter Eleven

London

London had been back in school for just a few days when she and Fatima decided to go ahead and really start the organization they'd been discussing for months and months. After plenty of late-night talks they each found out they'd both had drug addicts in their families or, in London's case, Amber. They both came to realize that drugs were tearing down neighborhoods and tearing families apart. They stayed up long nights after studying, coming up with a lot of key points that they wanted to cover in their meetings.

"I think we should make sure to focus on kids who don't get the food they need because their parents are on crack."

London was writing down both her and Fatima's ideas.

"Girl, I think we should try to shine the light on all the crime that senior citizens are subjected to by addicts trying to get money to cop." Fatima was on a roll with things to add on also.

London started to think about her friend Amber and came up with the last thing to put on the list. "Why don't we try to make the main focus on the youth, like kids in between nine and nineteen? If we can try to catch them, maybe we can make a difference. Tell them about another way to make it out the hood. Look how many of us are up here in school and can't look out or protect our little brothers and sisters from the dope man."

Fatima looked at London like she had just invented apple pie. "That's it! For real, for real. I think we just found our hook." Both girls were hyped up but decided to get some rest and get ready for a busy day.

Morning came quick enough, and the girls hurried to get dressed. "You ready, Fatima?"

"Yeah, almost, give me ten more minutes." London heard her say that and immediately thought about Kenya. She was always good for telling Gran that same line almost each and every morning.

Fatima grabbed her dorm room keys and the two were off. After a short walk across the campus, they cut across the football field, finally ending up at their destination. The girls made it to the school's media outlook building in what had to be record time. They were going to print out fliers to post all over the campus. London hoped that at least they would get ten or eleven people to show up at the group meeting that would be held on the weekend.

The day soon arrived and the girls were excited. "It's three o'clock. We have thirty minutes before everyone starts to get here. I'm so nervous." London was walking back and forth from the window to the door.

"Girl, we got this. I been hearing a few people talk about the fliers in class and in the computer lab." Fatima seemed to always know how to calm her friend down. "Just get up there and do the damn thang! Your ass is good at talking shit!" Fatima smiled as she hugged her roommate.

The meeting was about to start and, to the girls' surprise, it was standing room only. They had the dorm conference room packed to capacity with students. Some of their faces they knew on sight, and some of the people London and Fatima didn't even know attended the university.

"That flier must have been all kinds of powerful!" Fatima whispered to her soon-to-be partner in raising some hell.

London shook her head, agreeing. "I know, but I really think it just hit home with a lot of us. Let's get it started."

Fatima looked at London and knew her girl was gonna be definitely on point.

"Hello, everyone. My name is Amia London Roberts. I'm a freshman here and I have a few issues that trouble my mind at night. Hell, sometimes during the day." London had sparked some of the crowd's interest in what could be bothering such a pretty and well-spoken young lady. "It's my neighborhood at home. It's my little cousins and their friends, the ones who used to look up to me for guidance and even sometimes protection. Let me clarify: not protection from the physical side of the street, but the mental. The seemingly never-ending cycle of being hungry because Mom sold all of the food stamps for the month. The embarrassment of having to wear dirty or worn-out clothes to school, that is, if you ever had the encouragement to go." London was truly on top of her game and the entire room was hyped. "Look, I know many of you come from what we call 'the hood.' I bet you have brothers and sisters you worry about while attending school. We were lucky. Most of us had somebody in our lives. That one person who unconditionally cared about us and helped us, sometimes made us, make it through the tough times. All I'm saying is that just like we had that one shining beacon to guide us, it's time we stood up and let them pass the torch to us."

The crowd was on its feet. Fatima looked over to London and decided that she would not even speak. She knew that London would be the group's number one spokesperson from here on out.

The meeting went on for nearly two hours as each and every person gave their own story and personal account of what their issue was. Each one seemed to be worse than the last. At the conclusion of the first meeting, they decided on a name for the newly formed organization. It would be called People Against Illegal Drugs.

In short, PAID was formed and was officially ready to raise some hell for the youth. In London's words, it was time for change and the time was now!

Tastey

"Life is good as hell!" Tastey was feeling herself as she fell back on the bed in her hotel room surrounded by stacks and stacks of dough. Sure, most of it belonged to Zack, but a small cut of it was hers. She'd been stashing dope in the bottom of her dance bag for a little over a month now and getting paid. That meeting in Zack's office that night was paying off big time for her. Tastey had been stacking her loot from hustlin' and living off the tips she made from dancing. Her girl Raven went on the road with her from time to time whenever she could get a babysitter, so it was double the fun. The two of them would fall up in whatever strip club in the circuit they had to make a delivery to and practically take over that bitch. New girls, fresh meat as they were called, always made much more money than any of the regular girls on the roster. Tastey and Raven both were sexy as hell so snatching all the money wherever they went was never a problem. They knew how to give a nigga his money's worth. They were true showstoppers.

Zack, on the other hand, was starting to get nervous. Things were soon going to come to a screeching halt when his used-to-be longtime friend Stone got released and came home from prison, and he knew it. Stone stayed deep in Zack's pockets on an old debt Stone would never let him forget. As Zack sat down behind his desk, he looked at the pictures on the wall. One in particular stood out. It just so happened to be the same one that had jumped out at Tastey months earlier. It was like it was somehow calling out to him. Zack had had no idea whatsoever what Stone had wanted was so important that he had to send word by Young Foy to come see him in person. He often thought back to that day he fucked up, causing Stone to want to kill him dead. It would come to haunt him daily.

It was close to a three-hour ride up north to the penitentiary where Stone was housed. Zack went through all the normal procedures that it took to visit a friend or loved one. "Damn, this is some degrading bullshit!" he said out loud.

The guards just went on with their jobs. They were used to every type of verbal assault known to man or beast. Finally he got in and took a seat at a table. He then waited for what seemed like hours. The gate at the prisoner entrance finally cracked and Zack saw his old friend Stone bend the corner. Stone was looking hard faced, but that wasn't anything new to Zack; matter of fact that was how he originally had gotten that nickname: being stone-faced. They had grown up together in the same neighborhood and Stone barely smiled then either so Zack really made nothing of it at that point. As Stone got close to the table, he sat down. Obviously having something serious on his mind, he didn't bother or waste time even giving his boy any love.

"What dude, no dap, no love, what's up?" Zack was confused by this time. Each and every time his boy would do a bid, which was often, he would always accept his calls or send him some money on his books. He'd constantly looked out for him and his woman no matter what.

"*Man, I ain't gonna even front with you or spend no time with all that yang, yang. Dig this here! You know a young cat named Ty, a small-time car-thieving mother-fucker from DLA area? He 'bout twenty or twenty-one.*" Stone's face, being as it was, showed no signs of emotion as he spoke.

"*Yeah, I know him. He ain't 'bout shit,*" Zack eagerly chimed in. "*I know his bitch-ass wasn't showing no form of disrespect to you, was he? Because we stumped his ho-ass out awhile back for some bullshit.*"

"*Naw, not him! It's you, playa! You the one violating!*" Stone was mean mugging Zack like a motherfucker by this time, wanting to damn near smack the fire out his mouth. "*See that little punk was locked up here for a minute, doing a short stay. Ol' boy was talking mad shit about you: your boy Brother Rasul and that rotten cat house your slimy-ass run with Old Skool.*"

Zack was fucked up at the reckless way his boy was talking to him. Matter of fact he was straight-up offended. "*Damn, man, it was all good when you wanted to hang in the bitch. It keeps the bills paid on that phone you blow the fuck up and the money on your account. Where's all this hate from, dawg? I thought we was better than that.*"

Stone was boiling over with anger and could hardly stay in his seat. "*You right, flat out, guy! I thought we was better than that too. That's why I'm all fucked up. Please tell me that the ho-ass little nigga was lying and just trying to keep me from chin stumping his ass.*"

"*Come on, Stone, what you talking about? I'm lost.*" Zack was looking his longtime comrade in the face and waiting for some sort of explanation for his explosive anger.

Stone swallowed hard as hell and finally let it out. "*Dude, dig this here, I know you ain't got my little niece working in that joint, swing from no fucking pole?*" You *could almost see blood in Stone's eyes. Infuriated and enraged, his jaw was locked tight as he waited for a response to his question, or more like an accusation.*

"Niece! What niece?" Zack was stunned not knowing who or what he was talking about. "What the fuck are you talking about, man, and who the fuck?" The entire visiting room was starting to look over at the two of them as their voices rose.

"Ty told me you had my little niece Kenya up on stage showing her ass like some common tramp from around the way!" Out of his seat yelling at this point, Stone was ready to kill. "That's some foul-ass shit, nigga!" You could see the veins in his muscular arms start to swell, resulting in the guards quickly rushing over, trying to contain the commotion.

Zack was busy trying to explain to Stone that he had no idea that Kenya was his niece. "Oh shit! Damn, nigga! I didn't know that she was your family, I swear! I put that on everything! I'm sorry!"

Stone wasn't buying it and the guards had to drag him out the visiting room shouting the entire time. "I'll be out soon and on my brother Johnnie's grave, it's on, you feel me? You got his baby girl up there like that? You don't wanna see me, nigga, you don't want that!" The door slammed on Stone as he was still yelling, making a scene. Zack was left sitting at the table in shock over what he had just heard.

The phone started ringing, waking Zack up out of his trance. Daydreaming about that visit to the prison consumed most of his time. Haunting him, Zack also reminisced to back in the day when Stone had come to him needing some information about some young cats he'd turned his brother Johnnie on to. Zack didn't know that the guys he had just met that night were into sticking people up. They were flashing money around, claiming they were looking for some dope. How was he to know their true intentions? Even though Stone never came out and said it, Zack knew that a small part of him blamed him for his brother Johnnie's and his sister-in-law Melinda's heinous murders. After all, he did introduce them all. Whenever Stone would come around and bring up his deceased family members, Zack would automatically go in his pocket.

The guilt of what Stone had told him was killing his spirit. And now not only did he have his niece shaking her ass on stage, she was running dope, too. Zack prayed nightly that Stone would not make parole anytime soon. He knew that his now-former friend would be on a rampage and show little or no mercy.

"Hello." Zack had gotten in the habit of looking at the caller ID before answering the phone. Stone had him spooked. He was looking over his shoulder every moment, not knowing what to expect.

"Hey, Zack, it's me. It's all good my way." Tastey was still looking at the money that was thrown across the bed. She wished that all that cheddar belonged to her, but she had made her ends and was satisfied.

"Come on home, baby girl. I need to talk to you about something."

"About what?" she quizzed Zack, sensing a weird tone in his usually chipper voice.

Zack immediately cut her off. "You know I don't head bust about important shit on the phone. I'll just see you sooner rather than later."

"Okay, bet. No worries. I'll be home sometime in the early afternoon."

Zack had never mentioned his trip to the prison to visit Kenya's uncle. Vying for time, the money-hungry opportunist was trying to find another drug mule with as much street game as Kenya had, who could be trusted.

He was putting together a big deal that could bring him a huge payoff and then he could cut Tastey off and maybe pay Stone some major bread to stay off his ass. He would hate to see her go. It would be hard, but for his own personal safety there was no other way. Greedy, he knew he was already pushing his luck. But, the girl could hustle in the club and make shit happen in the streets. Realizing she was Johnnie Roberts's daughter, he knew she had that "get money or kill a nigga dead" DNA flowing in her bloodline. However, like it or not, the clock was ticking to let her go, and time was definitely not on his side.

Chapter Twelve

Tastey

It was about 1:45 in the afternoon when Kenya pulled up in the club parking lot. Heads Up had a lot of cars in the valet area, so she had to pull around to the side door. She called inside and had one of the guys on security have the door open. Kenya had more than $25,000 in her bag and didn't want to risk any fuckups by thirsty fools looking for a quick come up. She'd heard stories from old family friends about her parents slipping up that one time resulting in them getting murdered. Kenya, true to the streets, always tried to be on top of her hustle, no matter what it was.

"Hey, Young Foy! What's good?"

"Nothing, Tastey, just playing this work thing for a minute. You know how it is. A nigga still trying to get his music thang together and off the ground."

Young Foy let Tastey in the side entrance and personally walked her up to Zack's closed office door. On the way up the stairs, he mentioned to her that her ex-boyfriend Ty had been repeatedly calling up to the club asking for her.

"Man, fuck his ass. He ain't talking about shit I wanna hear! Last time he was up in here trying to front on a bitch, he got his shit split to the white meat!" Tastey was shaking her head from side to side, in true ghetto fashion, as she talked that talk.

"Yeah, I feel you, ma. Ain't no problem. I was just putting you up on it." Young Foy really liked Tastey, but he knew the upkeep on a female like her would hurt his pockets something serious. He knew a nigga on a budget couldn't keep a steady bitch, especially a bad bitch like Tastey. Young Foy left her to handle her business and made his way back on post.

"Hey, Old Skool. Hey, Zack." Tastey strolled in the office smiling and in good spirits as always.

"Hey, girl, we missed you around here." Old Skool ran across the room, hugging her tightly as if someone died.

Zack was both happy and sad. He knew if Tastey didn't go for this last big run, he'd be fucked in the game. Praying for the best, he smiled, hugging Tastey also.

Having had enough of the emotional couple, she placed her bag up on the table, opening it up. Old Skool went to lock the office door so they wouldn't be interrupted doing the count.

Tastey was beaming with pride. "It's all there. I didn't even take my cut out yet. I just counted it to make sure those niggas in Columbus ain't try no short change stuff!"

"I know you on top of it, baby girl. That's why I love your ass so much." Zack was happy to have that money in his hands. He knew that every trip was like a roll of the dice when it came to transporting, especially across state lines. Automatically, he slid Tastey three grand. Add that to the $850 she made dancing at the strip club she made the drop off at, and she had close to four grand. That was a hellava good night's work.

Tastey gathered her pay and was about to make tracks, when Zack stopped her. "Hold tight. I needed to discuss a proposition with you. I know it'll be worth your while."

"Well damn, let me take a seat. I've been driving all morning and still haven't eaten." Tastey, overly cautious, had to make sure to drive the speed limit and watch out for the state boys.

"Let me get you something from the kitchen. Sit your ass down and chill. You know I got you, baby." Old Skool listened to Tastey's order and took it down to the kitchen. It would give Zack time to hopefully work his game.

"Look, I'm gonna give it to you straight, like I always do. That trip you just came back from will more than likely be the last road trip I need you to make for me."

Tastey was tired as hell, but that statement from Zack woke her all the way up. "Dang gee, dude, why you saying that?"

"Girl, you've been on the highway making the same trips every few weeks. And I don't want them troopers to get familiar with seeing your face. I was thinking about letting the new girl, Spice, do her thang and make some extra money. She seems like good people." Zack could see the angry look on Tastey's face. "Look, sweetheart, I ain't trying to stop your flow. I'm only trying to look out."

"Yeah, I know, but I need to stack a little bit more loot." Tastey knew that the house that she and London jointly owned would hopefully be sold soon. When that happened, she wanted to have enough money to buy herself a little crib out in the suburbs, maybe even out of Michigan. To accomplish that, Kenya needed all the cash she could make, legal or illegal.

"I do have something else popping. It's kinda different from the driving thing."

Tastey was all in and Zack could tell. "Tell me what it is and what exactly I have to do."

"Well, first of all, are you scared to fly?" He leaned back in his chair, folding his arms.

"Naw, my people used to take me on trips when I was younger." Zack knew that she was talking about her uncle, his boy Stone. He got a chill when he even though about his name. "I ain't scared at all!" she blurted out like a G.

Zack explained to her that his buddy Deacon and his boy Storm had opened up a new strip club down in Texas named Alley Cats and he was trying to get a few girls from Detroit to bring some flavor to his place. Zack also went on to tell her that Deacon and Storm needed some product to move, so that they could finance some major remodeling they wanted to do.

"All you have to do is fly out there once, maybe twice, and it's a wrap. I'll pay you $5,500 for each trip."

"Damn, how much shit is it? I mean how much do I collect from Deacon, Storm, or whoever?" Tastey was all for it, but she had to see exactly how the program itself was supposed to play out.

Old Skool came back with her food and they all chopped it up, devising a solid game plan for Tastey. After talking and eating, Tastey headed home to take a long hot bath and think. She also was going to call her twin to check in on her. For some reason, the girls seemed to always miss the other's calls. London was submerged deep in her new life and Kenya wasn't hating. She was truly happy for her.

"Hey, Fatima. How you doing, girl?" Kenya was over all that silliness of being jealous of her sister's friendship with her roommate.

Fatima was also happy to hear Kenya's voice. She knew that London was starting to get worried about her twin because the two hadn't spoken in over a week, which seemed abnormal even in Fatima's eyes.

"Hey, Kenya, girl, we've been wondering where you been hiding out at. Let me run and get your sister. She's at the end of the hall, passing out some fliers for the upcoming meeting. You ought to come up and see your sister throwing down on her speeches. A lot of important people are going to be there. She's gonna blaze the stage, for real!"

"I ain't know ol' girl was getting at they heads like that. You make her sound like a li'l London X."

Both Fatima and Kenya giggled as Fatima waved down the hall to her roommate, holding the phone up. "She's on her way now. You grew up with the chic, you know she gotta get her last words in." Kenya was in total agreement with Fatima.

"Hello, this is Miss Roberts."

"Oh, damn. I ain't know we was all formal. Excuse the fuck outta me!" Kenya, teasing, was sounding uppity, snapping her fingers.

"Oh my God! Fatima didn't tell me it was you. She just handed me the phone, started smiling, and left out. Where in the hell have you been?"

"I've been around, here and there, Ohio, Chi-town, and a few days in upstate New York." Kenya was trying to play that shit off, but in reality, she thought she was Big Willie, low-key.

"I thought you fell your behind off the face of the earth. Don't you ever check your messages?" London wasn't going to let her twin sister get away with avoiding her calls without an explanation.

Kenya went into detail about Ty's visit up to her job and all the times that he called her house and the club. "Sis, I don't even listen to them crybaby messages he be leaving. I just push delete and keep on stepping. That crazy fool even left a letter on my car. I tore that shit up and threw it in the street, fuck even reading his bullshit. That nigga been a liar since conception!"

"Dang, what did you do to him? He seems like a stalker. You need to press charges against him or something." London was concerned for her sister's safety first and foremost.

"Yeah, you right, but forget his trick-ass. He got dealt with proper. Anyway, I heard you up there doing the damn thang." Kenya was hyping her sister up.

"Yeah, I guess you could say I'm doing a li'l some-thin'-somethin' as you say!"

Kenya was glad to know that all was well with London and she was doing big things. "So, I heard you got a big rally next weekend?"

London sighed. "Hey, why don't you come up and spend the whole weekend with me? I miss you."

"I wish I could, London, but I'm going to be in Texas and I don't know exactly when I might be back." Kenya hated disappointing her twin but business came first.

London was understanding of the situation, telling Kenya to do what made her happy. However, she had no idea that her sister was being a drug mule for the man their uncle considered partially to blame for their parents' untimely death. Kenya was part of the system that London was trying so hard to endlessly fight. London hated drugs and everything and everybody affiliated with them. Drugs made her and her sister orphans as far as she was concerned, and this was the outlook that she kept in the back of her mind whenever she made a speech.

"Well, London, I'm about to go to bed. I'm so tired that I'm about to fall asleep on this phone."

London hated to let her sister go, but was happy just to hear from her. "Hey, before you go, have you heard from Uncle lately?"

Kenya was apprehensive about talking about their uncle. Ever since she saw that picture of him in Zack's office, she had been avoiding his collect calls. Between him and Ty, she got used to turning the ringer off and pushing ignore. "He tried to call a few times, but I wasn't home. But if he calls you, tell him I still love him."

"Okay, then. I love you, Kenya."

Kenya lay back and smiled. "*Say U Promise!*"

***

Tastey

"You got everything packed the way we planned?" Zack was a little more than anxious about what was about to take place. With more than $65,000 worth of raw dope on the line, he took his time to go over the game plan repeatedly. "Listen up, Tastey, this is some major shit about to take place and we don't want or need any mistakes. Your freedom and my credibility is on the line. It took me and my people more than a week to negotiate on this deal. My people wants to take delivery of this shit almost as bad as I want to move it."

Tastey was trying her best to ease Zack's mind. "Be easy, I remember everything you said. The shit is twisted extra tight and double wrapped in triple plastic. Old Skool put cotton around it and then we put two more pieces of plastic. So chill, damn!"

"I ain't gonna be easy until your ass call me from the hotel telling me you made it." Zack was sweating, like he had to get on the plane with the dope his motherfucking self. "Matter of fact, I won't be happy until you meet up with Deacon and Storm and get my cash. I love them niggas like brothers and everything, but fuck the dumb stuff. I wanna see my money in hand. You feel me?"

"Listen, Zack, if you keep talking, I'm gonna miss my flight. You starting to mess with my good karma I got going on. Don't fuck my mind up. I need to be straight-up focused." Tastey was giving him a crazy look like, "Negro, please shut up!"

"Let her go. She's got her stuff together. You know that. When has she ever let you down?" Old Skool jumped in as she patted Zack on his back. "Relax!"

Zack watched Tastey and Brother Rasul pull out the parking lot and he wiped the sweat off his brow. In between letting that much dope out his sight and his con-science kicking his ass constantly about crossing Stone even though he knew the consequences, he was sick to his soul. Zack was losing weight and staying paranoid at the world and anyone in it.

After a long ride on a traffic-filled highway, Brother Rasul reached the airport. Tastey and he talked all the way there. "When I first met you, I knew it was something different about you, Sister Kenya."

Tastey was kinda thrown off because, it was the one and only time that he'd ever addressed her by her true real government name.

With conviction, he looked her in her eyes and spoke from his heart. "Have pride, young sister. Don't let the planted seeds of evil entice you from your true mission in life. Remember, I always got your back, even when you think I don't!"

Tastey grabbed Brother Rasul's hand and reassured him before she got out the car that this would be the only time that she'd be doing something this dangerous.

"Be safe, little sister, be safe." He headed back to the club to get ready for a long night filled with several reserved spot parties booked.

As Kenya made her way in the terminal at Detroit Metro Airport and checked her suitcases, she felt like all eyes were on her. Although she was used to being a star up on the stage, this was much different; her freedom was on the line.

"Now boarding at gate twenty-two, nonstop flight to Dallas," the lady on the loud speaker announced, causing a line to form at the gate.

Damn, that's me. This is it!

Tastey boarded the plane, found her seat, and got situated. *I wonder if they can tell I have all this shit stashed on me.* Her eyes followed everyone who got on the plane. Kenya got out a copy of a schoolbook and pretended to read, just like her and Zack planned. Getting even more into character, she even had on her State University hoodie that London had given her. If she could keep her cool, it would be all good.

After a bumpy ride and truly getting caught up in the banging novel, the plane finally landed and Tastey got off after gathering her belongings. She couldn't believe that she'd gotten away with it. She had even gotten so relaxed during the flight she took a nap.

I've got to find my luggage and get a cab. As she moved through the crowds of people, she felt at ease. The nervousness she was feeling earlier had passed. When she made it to the taxi stand, she thought, *Zack's boys must be some cheap-ass bastards. He could have sent a limo or something to pick me up,* not thinking that she could have drawn attention to herself.

Kenya got in the cab, telling the driver the hotel she had reservations at. The driver, claiming he made good time, made it to the hotel in less than twenty minutes. After paying the fare and tipping him an extra five, Kenya registered, got her key, and got to the room. She reached inside her purse and pulled out her cell phone.

Stone

Not more than ten minutes after Tastey bravely boarded the airplane heading to Dallas did her once-incarcerated uncle arrive back in the city after miraculously making parole. Young Foy, out in the streets checking his traps, saw Stone on the block as soon as his woman drove up to their house, and immediately stepped to him.

"Stone, my dude! What's good, God? When you touch down?" Young Foy gave his former bunkie some love while Stone's woman opened the trunk, grabbing the bag with her man's personal property in it.

"Just now. You know they can't hold a real hood warrior down. As hard as the white man put his foot down on my neck, the stronger I get." Stone stuck his chest out with pride, beating his clenched fist on his heart. "Real talk, I'm gonna go up in the crib, get some grub, take a bath, and hit these streets running." Stone headed up toward the door, focused on revenge. "I'll holler at you later. Oh yeah, and good looking on delivering that message to Zack for me. That was right on time."

"You know how we do, nigga! We family first and foremost! And if you need a li'l something in your pocket, I ain't got much, but you always welcome to half of whatever!"

"That's real, young blood, but I'm set. I'm 'bout to hit off some paper in a few! So, I'll holler!"

Young Foy looked at Stone's girl's ass swaying up the stairs behind Stone, and thought, *Fuck hittin' the streets. I'd be hittin' that ass!*

When Young Foy got to Heads Up to start his shift, annoyed, he saw Zack and Raven plotting over in a dark corner of the club. Young Foy, usually a player, had been spending a lot of time with Raven ever since he'd started working there. Surrounded by half-naked women nightly, he started kicking game to the single parent dancer, after he realized that he couldn't have Tastey. Raven, impressionable and loyal, was deeply in love with Young Foy; but he, on the other hand, wasn't exactly sure where his heart was truly at. Used to being classified as a dog, he was brand new when it came to the love game in general. All he knew for sure was music, slinging dope, and hustling; anything else was foreign.

"Hey now, Zack, what's the deal this evening, guy?"

Noticeably, his boss had a worried expression on his face. "Nothing, Young Foy, just seeing if Raven can text message Tastey for me about something." Without question, he was going to give himself a heart attack waiting to hear from his drug mule.

"Dig that," Young Foy responded, feeling uneasy about Zack being so cozy with his girl, boss or not.

Zack, having got Raven to text, then excused himself. "Well, let me go to my office. I have some things to take care of. I'll see you two in a minute." As Zack turned to walk away, Young Foy unknowingly threw some salt in the game, asking him if he was going to block off a VIP section for his old friend Stone.

Dry mouthed, Zack quickly turned white as a ghost. "What you mean, block off for Stone?" He was sweating bullets, waiting for Young Foy to answer the question.

"Come on, dude. I know you knew your man was coming home, didn't you?" Young Foy gave him a strange look, wondering why Zack was acting so shocked.

Zack tried to play it off, not wanting to seem like he was out the loop as he pumped him for information on the sly. "Yeah, um, I did. Have you heard from him yet?"

"Yeah, actually, I just ran into him and his girl around the way. He was just touching down."

When Zack heard that Stone was released from prison, his heart started to pound extra fast. Interrupting their conversation, his cell phone then suddenly started to ring and scared the shit out of him. He looked at the screen and ran up to his office to take the call.

"Damn, what's up with that?" Raven asked Young Foy as she kissed him softly on the lips.

"I don't know what's up with his ass. That guy been bugging out for the past few weeks now." Raven and Young Foy laughed together as Zack entered his office, slamming the door shut behind him.

Tastey

"Hey, Zack, I'm here! What took you so long to answer the phone?" Tastey was kicking her shoes off, getting ready to take a long bath and relax her nerves.

"I was down in the club handling some business. Is everything okay your way? Did you have any problems? Are you at the hotel?" Zack quizzed her as if he was conditioning a full-scale interrogation.

Tastey was not trying to get stressed the fuck out by his worrying and overthinking shit. "Listen, I'm here in the hotel. It's room 1369 and I'm tight!"

Zack had to think quickly, considering the bad news that Young Foy had just given him. Naturally he didn't want Tastey to come back to town with all his money in tow and Stone was out walking the streets, possibly running into her before he had a chance to explain his side of what happened to her parents that God-awful night. Zack was confused, to say the least, knowing damn well it was just a matter of time before Stone, who was out for blood, would be paying him a visit. "Dig this here, Tastey. It's been a slight change in plans. My boys Deacon and Storm have to hustle up on a little bit more loot. So I need you to chill in Dallas one more day, on my pockets, of course. As soon as they get their situation together, you and them can bump heads. Oh, and by the way, I don't want you to call me anymore until you three meet. I don't want any phone traces back here from the police or something. The next call you should get will be from one of them; Deacon or Storm." Zack had to buy himself some time to try to reason with Stone, and keeping his niece under wraps would have to do for now.

"All right, Zack, not a problem. I guess I could go to the mall or catch a movie. I'll be fine. Don't worry about me. I'm good. I'll wait for the call and take care of that. Talk to you in a few days." Tastey hung up the phone and placed it on her charger. Happy to spend on someone else's tab, she ran her bathwater and took out an outfit to wear to the mall.

Zack called Brother Rasul up to the office, informing him that he wanted extra security in the club for the next few days.

Brother Rasul, sensing his crooked boss and friend had once again dug himself deep into a twisted weave of bullshit, suspiciously rubbed his chin. "All right then, but what's wrong? I can tell you've been acting strange the last couple of weeks or so."

"Listen, Ra, you been with me since I first opened these doors. You already know I trust you with my life, so I got you. Just let me try to figure a few things out and I'll fill you in later. For now, just beef shit up a little—quick."

Zack knew Ra was his boy and would be up on top of having his back; he always was. Brother Rasul was probably Zack's only true friend he had left in the world, even though he didn't deserve his friendship or loyalty. Zack put on a good front, but he was a real snake, low-key, and everyone who came in contact with him knew it.

Chapter Thirteen

Brace Up

Tastey awoke from the nap that she had taken when she got out the tub. Slipping on a soft pink sundress and a pair of sandals that showed off her perfectly polished toes, she stashed the bag containing the dope and pulled the door closed, hanging a DO NOT DISTURB sign. After stepping off the elevator, she made her way through the lobby feeling like she had life by the tail. All the men turned their heads to watch her ass bounce from side to side with each step. The cab ride was interesting, as she saw a lot of different sights. Dallas was a lot different from Detroit. Being in a brand-new environment made Kenya yearn for a change in her own.

As she entered the mall, the air conditioning in the building was on full blast and you could see her hardened nipples poking through the thin cloth of her dress. A seasoned veteran in shopping, Kenya went in and out of all of the stores in the mall and was soon loaded down with all sorts of bags. She had everything from True Religion, Prada, and Gucci to Armani and Ralph Lauren. Strolling like she owned the world, the diva born and raised in Detroit felt like she was reenacting a scene straight out of the movie *Pretty Woman*. Going into the Versace boutique, normally aware of her surroundings, she didn't notice two guys on the men's side of the shop staring at her. The brown-skinned taller man of the two was mesmerized by her swag.

Kenya took her time browsing through the rack and saw a navy blue suit that was calling her name. She struggled with her bags as she held the outfit up to her body, staring into a floor-length crystal-framed mirror.

"Hello, miss, I'm Nyasha. Would you like to try that on?" The saleslady was very polite and wanted nothing more than to make a commission on the sale of a $950 suit.

"Yes, please." Tastey gave the salesgirl her other bags to put out of the way and entered the dressing room. After carefully fastening the buttons and zipping up the skirt, she exited the fitting room, hoping for a reaction. Once again, all eyes were on Kenya just as she thought. The two guys who had been watching her were both in awe, as well as several other customers.

"Wow, it fits you perfectly. Not everyone has the body shape to pull this suit off like you do." Nyasha wanted to make the sale and nine out of ten times would lie to make it, but this time it was no lie. Kenya was killing it in the suit.

"It is pretty, isn't it?" Tastey turned around in the mirror several times before returning into the fitting room to change back into her sundress. After looking at the price tag and realizing that it was way too much to pay for an outfit that she'd probably never get to wear, she felt sad. It was too much of a classy outfit for her lifestyle. Hesitantly, she handed it to the saleslady over the shuttered door to restock, and finished getting dressed. Making her way back up to the counter to get her other bags and thank the lady for being so helpful, all of a sudden the saleswoman asked her to sign the receipt.

"What are you talking about? I'm sorry. I'm not going to buy the suit today," Kenya insisted, throwing her hand up. The saleslady giggled as she saw one of the guys who were watching her customer approach them.

"You don't have to buy it, pretty lady. I already purchased it for you!" the handsome guy boldly interrupted.

Kenya, knowing you could never get something for nothing, was in shock and of course suspicious of his motives. "I'm sorry but you don't even know me. Why would you do something so random like that? What's the catch?"

"Well, I can easily fix that. My name is Tony Christian." He reached out his hand to shake hers. "And it ain't no catch. I just wanted you to have it! Is it wrong for a man to give a woman a gift? Is that a crime?"

It was then when she noticed his iced-out watch and ring. He had a linen outfit on and gator sandals to match. By the way the generous man's clothes fit, it looked like he worked out every single day. Kenya was in a daze staring at him. She shook herself together and took his hand. "Hello, my name is . . . Kenya." She decided that this wasn't the club, so all that "Tastey" shit could be ceased for the time being.

"Listen, can we go have lunch and talk for a while? I noticed that you didn't have a ring on your finger."

Kenya was impressed with his smooth demeanor. "Yeah, I guess so. I am kinda hungry," she blushingly accepted the invitation.

Tony helped Kenya with her bags, including her new suit, and the two left the store. He signaled for his boy to come over to where he and Kenya were standing. "Kenya, this is my little brother O.T." After Tony made the introductions, they all walked toward the food court. He couldn't take his eyes off her. "I would take you somewhere a little bit more upscale, but I know you might feel a little somewhat uneasy, seeing how we just met and all." Storm was used to going first class or not going at all. He knew if given a chance he would really take Kenya out on the town and floss.

They talked for almost an hour before O.T. excused himself and left. He made sure to tell his brother to call him later because they had a meeting to attend. O.T. liked Kenya, she seemed cool, but he knew his brother was acting all in. O.T. could tell by the look in his eyes that he wasn't going to let this female go. Shit, besides, Mr. Christian was already $950 in the hole being a cake.

"So listen, can I take you out for a real meal tonight?" Storm knew he was pressing his luck, but he felt like he'd known her forever.

Kenya, strange as it seemed, had the same vibe about him. She had flown to Dallas for strictly business, but in a matter of minutes, it got extremely personal. "Well, I think that can be arranged. After all, you are the only person I know in town." Kenya told him a quick lie and led him to believe that she was in town to interview for a job.

Tony's cell phone kept ringing. "I'm sorry, Kenya. I have an important meeting to attend and I can't be late. Can I drop you off at your hotel? You have my word, I don't bite." He smiled and melted her young soul.

They gathered the bags and made their way through the mall and over to the valet entrance. Tony handed the guy his ticket, as he and Kenya both stared into one another's eyes until the valet attendant pulled up with his car.

"This us, ma!" He put her bags in the back seat and like a real gentleman he held the door open for Kenya.

"Damn, what the fuck?" she whispered softly under her breath. "This nigga pushing a Benz CLK55, buying $950 hookups, and buying a bitch dinner later, this guy is straight up ballin'!"

After a short ride, she was in front of the hotel. Tony pulled out a big knot of money and peeled off a twenty, paying the doorman to make sure that all of Kenya's bags were taken up to her room. He then smoothly leaned over, opened the glove compartment, and pulled out a card. "Take this number and call me when you get ready."

Kenya scooted over and kissed him on his cheek like some old junior high bullshit. "Thanks again for the outfit."

"Don't thank me, just do the right thing and call me!" He winked his eye, blowing her a kiss.

As she walked away Kenya made sure to put a little bit extra in the way she moved her hips.

Damn, I got to have her! His dick immediately got hard as he drove away caught up in his emotions.

Chapter Fourteen

The Plan

"Hey, man! Thanks for coming over on such short notice to have a nigga's back." Stone greeted a couple of his boys he'd hooked up with during one of his various bids in the penitentiary. Charlie Moe and B-Rite were both ruthless criminals with no conscience for wildin' the fuck out. When Stone called, they were more than happy to show up and show out for their comrade. The three men had formed a bond after beating down a snitch on the prison yard. They beat the guy within an inch of his life. No one in or out of the joint liked a snitch.

"Whatever we can do. You know I'm ready to ride." B-Rite raised his shirt up, pulling out his gun. He took the clip out and checked the bullets one by one. Charlie Moe followed almost the same routine, as he yanked his shit out of his waistband.

Stone gave both his boys a dap and started to explained the situation to them. "Let me tell you what the deal is. A bitch-ass nigga named Zack, who first got my brother set up and murdered back in the day, got my young niece showing, spreading her legs open up in his spot. I'm through tolerating his foul-ass!"

"Dawg, let's stretch his ass proper!" Charlie Moe was hyped to tear some shit up. With him killing was never a problem, but more like a hobby.

Stone instructed both his friends to meet him inside of Heads Up at about 7:30 p.m. and come ready to put in that work. "Y'all make sure to wear your Muslim garb so that way you can get your heaters in. The cat at the door is all about Islam, and nine out of ten times he would never disrespect you by asking to search your garments."

The trio went over the game plan as they downed a couple of forties that Stone's woman had brought in from the kitchen.

Zack

"Hey, baby!" Old Skool greeted Zack as he made his way inside the club doors. She was sitting at the bar, watching Young Foy eat the dinner that Raven had cooked for him. She couldn't help but wish that she and Zack could go back to the time that he was in love with her, but he'd made it perfectly clear on more than several occasions his feelings had changed. However, Old Skool was still in love with him and that feeling would never die. "I said hey, baby! What's the matter with you? Didn't you hear me?"

Zack stopped, giving her a slight hug. "Oh, I'm sorry, my bad. I got a lot on my mind." He wanted to tell somebody about just how fucked up he was really living, but his pride wouldn't let him. He wanted to announce he'd been looking over his shoulder, terrified to breathe all day long, but couldn't. "Look, I'm gonna go up to my office. I'll be back down later. I need to make some calls and handle a few things." Zack held his head down as he walked up the stairs.

Brother Rasul, doing what he did, came over to get the roster of girls who would be working that night, so he could post his best security around the big moneymakers. The club had two bachelor parties booked and he wanted to make sure that everything went smoothly on the shift. One was a bunch of young cats from the factory and the others were a group of fake, uppity, wannabe white Uncle Tom educators who thought they were doing the club and the dancers a huge favor by coming and spending their money in the hood instead of in a white club.

"All right, fellas! Let's give this next lady some love. She has enough shake in the ass to make a blind man see! Enough junk in the trunk to a make a crippled man walk, and even bring Tupac out of hiding!" The crowd erupted in laughter at the DJ. "I'm looking for the one they call Raven!"

The club was full, energy level on bump, and the crowd was hyped. Both bachelor parties were in full swing and everyone there were getting their drink on. Having double-checked to make sure Kenya, aka Tastey, wasn't working at the club that evening for sure, all systems were go in the plan Stone laid out. B-Rite and Charlie Moe had both easily gotten into the club without being checked. They even stood at the front door, kicking it with Brother Rasul for a good ten minutes or so about where they prayed at and mutual friends they shared. Him being able to recognize them meant nothing at this point in time, because nine outta ten, Charlie Moe and B-Rite knew Brother Rasul; if he chose to step up and go for bad, they wouldn't live to see daybreak anyhow. They didn't give a shit what Muslim renegade group he was affiliated with. They also had their boys posted throughout the club and made sure that they'd handed off pistols to each one of them, having all angles covered when the festivities of revenge started.

Zack walked over to his office wall and snatched down the picture of Stone, throwing the snapshot in the trash.

Fuck being scared! Stone don't want none with me! Let me get this call over with! Zack was trying to be brave and think positive, but he wasn't even fooling his own self. Zack sat behind his desk and dialed Deacon's cell phone number and waited for him to answer.

"Hey, dude, what up, man? I've been waiting for you to hit me up." Deacon was anxious to get started in their impending venture and new-formed partnership. "Me and ol' boy are about to meet up in a few minutes. We're definitely ready!"

Zack had to get the tradeoff over and get his money home as soon as possible. He was a nervous wreck and hadn't slept well in days. This shit was taking a serious toll on his health. His hands shook as he held the phone. "My people are already in town. Dial this number and ask for Tastey. You two can decide on the drop-off location. I don't need any short shit, Deacon! I got a lot riding on this!" Zack added extra bass in his tone as if he could really reach out and touch someone.

Deacon reassured Zack that their revenue was right and he had his best people on top of it. The two then went over a few minor details before they ended the conversation. Zack then went inside his private bathroom to splash cold water on his face before he went downstairs to play host for the evening. *It's all good. I ain't fazed,* he repeated relentlessly in his mind, still trying to convince himself of the lie.

Mayhem

It was 7:25 p.m. and Stone was getting out of his girl's car. He was more than ready to confront Zack on the grimy shit he'd done once again to his family. This was the day he'd been waiting for ever since Ty put him up on the disrespectful situation concerning Kenya. He'd been trying to call Kenya every day for over a month or so and couldn't get an answer to hear her side of the story. Stone didn't want to send his woman to handle his family business. That just wasn't his style. He also had no idea that Ty, too, had been trying to get in touch with his niece to warn her about him finding out. Ty, just like Stone, had been leaving message after message with no response.

Nevertheless, it was time for Zack to finally shake hands with the devil. Stone reached the front door and cracked his knuckles before he opened it up. He could hear the loud music and the sounds of the crowd, laughing, cheering and having a good time. *All this hee-hawing 'bout to cease when I get up in this joint. That's my motherfucking word!* Stone entered the club trying not to look suspicious. His first sight was Young Foy, who, luckily, was working the front door. It was right then and there he knew that getting his gun inside would be no problem at all.

"What's good, God? I told that nigga Zack that he should've blocked you off a VIP section." Young Foy leaned in and hugged his friend. Automatically, he felt Stone's gun on his hip, but thought nothing of it. After all, he knew Stone was Zack's homeboy from way back when, and always received special treatment whenever he was on deck wherever he went.

"Oh naw, I'm tight on that. I'm just gonna grab a seat at the bar, get a quick drink, then bounce."

Stone stepped all the way inside door. He stood at the front of the club quickly scanning the crowd. He first saw B-Rite in a corner booth, followed by one of his crew posted by the stairway. After making eye contact with them, he walked past Charlie Moe and two other cats nodding at them. They all were in place and the shit was going as planned. The only holdup was Zack's punk-ass. He would be the star of the show tonight, not the half-naked strippers. Stone ordered a rum and Coke and waited for the shit to go down.

Old Skool was sitting at the far end of the bar with Brother Rasul counting the number of girls and who hadn't paid the house fee yet. It was a busy night, which always led to plenty of confusion.

"Let me get back on post. Do me a favor and send some juice over to my Muslim friends who came in. They're sitting over there in that booth waiting to meet up with some people." He pointed over toward B-Rite and Charlie Moe.

Brother Rasul had no idea that they were not friends and hadn't come in peace. Although their presence in the club bothered him, he wasn't representing Islam to the fullest by being there either. The entire night so far was leaving him uneasy for some strange reason. The usual strong-minded individual was a little thrown off his square. Between worrying about both Tastey, who was out of town, and Zack hiding a secret, his mind wasn't focused. This job was taking a toll on him and his spirituality.

Old Skool never looked up as she replied, "All right, Ra, as soon as I finish the count I'll have the juice sent right over." She had her mind focused on collecting from every dancer that night; no more weak excuses. Some of the slick, ghetto-raised females were starting to fall off of paying and it was her job to be on top of it. Old Skool never liked to let Zack down. She knew that her longtime lover worshipped money and she always wanted to bless him with as much as she could get.

As the evening got into full swing, there was a growing crowd of fellas at the entrance waiting to get inside. Per club policy, each one had to get patted down and searched for any weapons or bottles they'd try to sneak inside. Heads Up was almost at capacity level. Brother

Rasul went back up to the front door to switch spots with Young Foy, who was more than happy to get back to the floor so that he could watch his woman Raven handle her business. Some of the guys who were with the wannabe white bachelor party were getting a little rough with the dancers. The out-of-control few were ordering bottles of champagne and acting wild, breaking all the strict house rules they felt they could get away with. Several of the bouncers had already argued with them, warning of the consequences. The group of drunk and disorderly men was well on their way to getting thrown out of Heads Up for the night, which was fine with Young Foy.

"Hey! Whoa! Please don't grab me like that. You're hurting me!" Raven was trying to reason with the man from the group she was giving a lap dance to. He was yanking at her long weave and trying to feel in between her legs.

"Look, I'm giving you twenty dollars for a few minutes' worth of work. Now stop your annoying bitchin', you uneducated little slut!"

The man possessed a sinister look in his eye. Young Foy was getting pissed off as he angrily stared at them. It was at that moment in time he realized just how much he really did love Raven and her small son. Feeling some sort of way, he decided he would tell her later that night. Young Foy was ready to settle down, and he was sure Raven was the one. However, his blood pressure was shooting straight up as he watched the older man disrespect his woman. *This nigga got one more minute before I say fuck this job, and beat his ho-ass!* Young Foy thought as he rubbed his hands together and his heart raced.

Zack cracked opened his office door and heard the sounds of people spending money. *Damn, I gotta get downstairs and play host. Time for me to shine!* In spite of being sick from worry about Stone making good on his promises, he still had a club to run. After all, he was the boss and had to keep his fronts up no matter what the price was.

Getting it together, Zack fixed his tie and headed down the stairs, trying his best to overcome his fear. With the eye of a hawk, he looked across the entire club for any signs of anything abnormal. As far as he could tell, it was packed. Everything seemed normal and everyone appeared to be having a good time. That meant he was making money, so he was happy. But like they say, all good things must come to an end. Well, this was about to be one of those times in Zack's otherwise perfect life.

Stone sat inconspicuously perched on a barstool on the other side of the room. Feeling unstoppable, he saw Zack, dressed in a suit and tie, make his way slowly down the staircase. His blood started to boil. Stone could feel his heart pumping overtime as he also watched some of, if not all of, the dancers degrade themselves like he knew Kenya was doing as well. As the clock ticked, his adrenalin rose. This would be his ultimate revenge for having his niece whore herself out for a few dollars, and his long-coming payback for both her parents' murders. Stone swallowed the last bit of his drink he was nursing and stood up, brushing his pants off. That was the signal for Stone's crew that it was getting ready to go down. Zack was his, and any wannabe heroes, on staff or not, his cohorts who were riding with him would deal with. It was on! It was show time!

"Hey, Old Skool, sweetheart. How's the count on the girls and the door going? How we looking?" Zack was so engrossed in finding out about the dollar amount that he didn't observe Stone creeping up behind him. Old Skool noticed Stone first and smiled. She knew all of Zack's boys.

"Hey, baby. I was wondering when you were coming down to join us. When did . . . ?" Before Old Skool could finish greeting him, her smile quickly turned into her jaw damn near dropping to the strip club floor.

Zack, already nervous and jumpy as a cat, saw the expression on her face. Praying first, he eased his body around just in time to see Stone push his newly shined 9 mm pistol dead in his face. Zack, terrified, wasted no time with being humble, trying his best to cop a plea. "Let me explain, Stone. Hold up! I can pay you! Wait! Please don't do this!" Zack was begging for his life knowing the pedigree of his longtime associate and what he was capable of if pushed to it.

Stone, not caring about the multitudes of witnesses, had to laugh at his former friend, Zack, who always tried to go for bad every chance he got. "Don't do what, moth-erfucker? You ain't shit but a store-bought pimp. Look at you! You fuckin' little pussy! You thought it was okay what you got my niece doing up in this motherfucker?"

"Niece?" Old Skool puzzled with tears in her eyes.

"Shut the fuck up, Old Skool. This murder about to take place right here is between two grown-ass men!"

Zack was paralyzed with fear as he faced his future. It was certain death as Stone nudged the barrel of the gun to his temple. "Naw, man, please hold up! I told you I didn't know Kenya was Johnnie and Melinda's daughter! I told you that!"

"Please don't, Stone!" Old Skool begged for mercy, shocked at who Stone was claiming Kenya truly was. "Please don't! For old time's sake don't!" All the nights the three of them spent in the club drinking meant nothing to Stone at this time. He was in a zone of his own.

"Shut the fuck up, you ancient, sagging-titty bitch! I done told you this is between me and this ho-ass nigga here!" He spat directly in her face, leaving her stunned.

Stone was hyped and drunk with power as he humiliated his prey. Zack had tears in his eyes and warm piss was running down his right pants leg. "Now straighten your tie and boss up!" Stone laughed out loud and, without a second thought about the crowd of shocked onlookers, ruthlessly pulled the trigger. "Damn, my nigga! Ain't no fun when the rabbit got the gun. Is it, bitch!" Stone emptied his entire clip into Zack's body. Feeling smug with no remorse, he then watched his former friend collapse onto the floor. "You already suited and booted for a funeral, casket ready, so it's whatever!"

Old Skool had blood splattered across her dress and face. She screamed over and over again as she held Zack's limp and lifeless body close. "No! No! No!" she sobbed uncontrollably in the middle of what had become chaos.

At that point, all hell broke loose and shots were fired from every direction possible. In the midst of the pandemonium, Brother Rasul pulled both guns out, which he always carried, ready for war. Fearlessly, he ran into the crowd of hysterical people toward Zack's assailant, Stone. B-Rite, being the loyal goon he was paid to be, saw the direction his Muslim brother was headed in and let off several rounds. Good with his aim, three bullets hit their mark, knocking Brother Rasul off his feet and into the side of several chairs. On the other side of the club Raven, terrified like the rest of the innocent dancers, was trying to get off of the disrespectful man's lap she was giving a dance to. Using all her strength, she fought, struggling to get away and to safety, but couldn't. The man was cowardly holding Raven close to him like a shield from the gunfire.

Young Foy, having the heart of a lion, was jumping over chairs to rescue Raven from harm's way. He made it less than two feet from her when a parade of more shots recklessly rang out inside the strip club walls. Shockingly he saw one of the bullets tear through Raven's back. All of her movement and attempts to break free from the man's hold abruptly stopped. The customer who was holding Raven coldly let her limp body fall to the broken glass floor without so much as a second thought. When the spineless man looked up to make his escape from any more stray bullets that were flying, he was face to face with Young Foy, who raised his pistol and made the coward meet his Maker. The street-born and raised youth made sure the older dude, who had just proven himself to be less than a man, was sure to have a closed-casket funeral. Young Foy felt his heart break in two as he looked at Raven, knowing she was gone. He then laid his body on top of hers, shielding it, to make sure that she didn't get hit again.

All of Stone's crew had made it safely to the door and he was almost there also. People, not know which way to go or turn, were screaming, taking cover in every corner of the bar they could hide. Charlie Moe yelled out to Stone to hurry the fuck up. He knew that the police would soon be on their way and no one on the team wanted to go back to prison, at least not tonight. Stone dumbly had used all his ammunition laying Zack down and was now at a total disadvantage to defend himself. Bullets were flying in every direction and sheer panic and pandemonium were taking over the club. When Stone finally reached the door, he was suddenly stopped by a hot, burning sensation rushing throughout his entire body. Everything started to move in slow motion to him. He was getting weak and felt dizzy. Stone fell to the ground and looked up to see Old Skool standing over him with a smoking gun at her side.

"Why? Why did you do it, Stone? I know he was a snake, but I loved him!" Tears were streaming down her face, causing her eye makeup to run down her cheek like a sad raccoon. Old Skool screamed out loud in anguish and shot Stone once more, ripping a gaping hole in his chest. *What else is left?* she thought before turning the gun on herself, choosing not to live life without her man.

Chapter Fifteen

London

London had been working on her speech for the entire week, wanting to make sure it was perfect. Tonight would be her first time speaking in front of a packed auditorium, filled with not just students, but most of the professors, the deans, and a few politicians, all who wanted to attach themselves to the fast-growing antidrug movement Fatima and London founded. The media was set up on the side of the stage and the lights beamed brightly. The crowd was constantly growing, as they were all anticipating London's inspiring, heartfelt words. She already had a loyal following who related to the message she and her organization were trying to get out.

"Girl, I can't believe all these folks are out here. I know we wanted a big turnout, but dang!" London had to try to calm herself down. It was a little bit overwhelming for an orphaned twin from the ghetto to grasp.

Fatima asked one of the people backstage to please get London a glass of water. "Listen, London, you got this. We've been passing out fliers and cards for close to two weeks now. Everyone is exited. Everyone is motivated. And last, but not least, everyone is tired of drugs ruining their neighborhoods. Go do your thang. They're waiting for you!"

After listening to Fatima give her a pep talk, London was motivated, ready to move the crowd. "Ladies and gentlemen, students, professors, and distinguished guests, I want to welcome you to the first ever 'Take Our Kids Back' rally, sponsored by PAID!" The crowd started to clap and everyone was hyped as London continued, "For those of you who don't know what PAID is, it's an organization that was formed by a group of students, such as myself, who are sick and tired of getting phone calls from our parents about the trouble that our little brothers and sisters are getting into. We're tired of our family not being able to walk to the candy store without being harassed!" London took another drink of water. "Smoking crack, shooting dope, or sniffing cocaine, what-ever their choice of high is, is certainly not our choice. We want to be left out of the world that these people bring to our children. Kids don't deserve to live in poverty and total despair!" The audience was in a trance of total agreement as they listened to London speaking. "Black-on-black crime is at an all-time high, because most of us only know destitution. It's a complete injustice to children, of all races and nationalities, to be continuously subjected to being hungry, being scared to walk to school, being ignored by their drug-addicted parents, and feeling like no one cares!" Every one of the people in attendance was standing on their feet and cheering.

Fatima was holding London's bag and couldn't turn off her cell phone, which kept ringing. After about three times of the phone ringing, back to back, she finally answered it. Fatima was having trouble trying to hear what the caller was saying, so she went out the side door of the building where it was somewhat quieter.

"Hello, hello." Fatima listened to the caller speak and instantly began to panic. "No, this is her roommate! Oh my God! She's on stage!" Fatima was almost in tears in the middle of the conversation. "As soon as she walks off I'll have her call you right back. Is this the number where you're at?" Fatima, frazzled, waited for the woman on the phone to respond and then closed the phone up. She ran back in the auditorium, just as London was finishing up her speech.

"I don't have the luxury to have a lot of money. I can't just pick up and move to what people say is a better block or neighborhood. Let's not move. Let's take back our kids and our community!" London took another sip of water and continued. "I ask every person here today to get involved. Write to your local politicians and demand that legislation be passed to help our kids. Start policing your own community. PAID is going to start chapters at each and every campus that we can. Please pick up the literature at the back tables, and thank you for coming out."

The cheers from the crowd could be heard from outside of the building and all over campus. Some of the people in the audience were moved to tears. The excitement and waves of emotion from them filled the air. As London walked off the stage making her way through the many people congratulating her on the speech, she spotted Fatima running toward her. She had tears in her eyes that London quickly noticed as Fatima got closer.

"What's wrong with you? What happened?"

Fatima quickly pulled London out the side door so they could have some privacy and talk. "Listen, while you were on stage you got a phone call. There's been an accident and we've got to get you home!"

"Accident? What do you mean, accident?" The first thing London thought about was Kenya and that club. "Is she all right? Is she okay? I knew that club wasn't any good and would get her in trouble!"

Fatima saw that London was bugging out and tried her best to calm her down. "Slow down, London, and pay attention. It's not Kenya. She's okay, I assume. It's your uncle, Stone. He's been shot. We gotta get back to Detroit as soon as possible! Now hurry, come on!"

London stopped dead in her tracks. She was confused. "My uncle? But what are you talking about? He's in jail. How did he get shot in jail? Did he try to escape or something?" London was holding her head by this time, in utter shock.

Fatima gave London the number where she could reach the woman who had called with the tragic information. After London dialed the number and spoke to her uncle's woman, they rushed back to the dorm room, gathered some things, and jumped in Fatima's car, heading to Detroit. No soon had they gotten on the highway than London pushed in the numbers to Kenya's cell phone, praying that her twin sister would answer and hopefully shed some light on what was going on at home.

Tastey

Kenya was happy to be back in her hotel room so that she could try on all the new clothes that she'd bought. As she pulled the outfits out one by one, she started to smile. Thinking about the suit that Tony purchased for her made her insides get warm. She closed her eyes while remembering the smell of the cologne he had on and the his soft cheek. It made her want to run to the phone and tell him to turn back around, come up to her room, and fuck the shit out of her. It had been more than a minute since the last time she had gotten some and Tony's athletic body had the potential to be just what the doctor ordered. Kenya was getting wet just imagining.

Deacon had just hung up the phone. He and his partner Storm had been anticipating Zack's call for days. It was finally time for them to start to really blow up on their own, independent of any local connect who was cutting the product off jump. Deacon was small-time hustling since he was a teenager and had to spend every dime that he'd saved to open up his new club. His hope was to make Alley Cats the most popular strip club in Texas. Deacon didn't have any cash left in his stash when almost complete with the project, so his boy, a boss in his own right had his back. Deacon wasn't broke, but his cash flow was tapped out; that's why he needed Storm to come in on the deal.

When Zack got in touch with him with what was a deal of a lifetime, he and Storm had to jump on it. Storm, just like having his back for extra revenue for the club, still was holding hard. He was making some major chips and Deacon knew he was one of the only dudes in the city who had that type of cheese readily available. He knew that Storm would definitely want in on the deal. He was all about making money.

"Yo, my nigga! I was just wondering when you would show up. Your brother got here about a half hour ago. He told me you was out chasin' that cat." Deacon had a huge grin on his face as he let his boy inside the door.

"Never that guy. I don't chase cat, cat chase me. Fuck what you heard!" Storm was holding his nuts, while both Deacon and O.T. made fun of him. "Y'all busters up in here fooling, hell, I might just make ol' girl wifey. Why you bullshitting? Ask O.T., that guy seen her ass. She's right with hers!" Storm was serious and they could tell. He was putting a deep bass in his tone as he spoke. "Deacon, I'm telling you, she's badder than any of these cum-drunk broads you got pole slanging up in this bitch!" He continued to campaign on Kenya's behalf, until he saw that all he was getting in response was laughter. Storm then grabbed the darts that were on the bar and started throwing them extra hard at the board.

"Listen, guy, I ain't mad at you. Do what you feel, but a nigga like me gonna keep a ho selling my half of the pussy! Matter of fact her half too! Ask my girl Paris, she'll tell you. I'm about that bread!"

All three of them fell out at O.T.'s crazy wannabe pimp-ass. Ready to handle business, the trio sat down, counting up all the money Deacon and Storm had put aside for their impending deal with Zack. When they made sure the count was correct, Deacon reached over the bar, getting the cordless phone. "Let me make this call and set this thing into motion." Deacon dialed the number Zack had just given him and waited for someone to answer. After three rings, a sexy-sounding female answered.

"Hello." Kenya saw the area code on her caller ID and knew it was the call that she was waiting for.

"Yeah, can I speak to Tastey?"

"This me. Who is this?" She automatically got into gangsta mode.

"This is Deacon. Can we meet up soon?" He started to pace the floor, anticipating making money. Storm and O.T. went behind the bar and each grabbed two beers, waiting for Deacon to get the tradeoff location.

"Damn, I wonder if she is tasty." O.T. licked his lips as he opened his bottle.

Tastey looked at all her bags and thought about the only place that she knew how to get to in town and suggested the mall. Deacon quickly agreed.

"I'll tell you what. I'm gonna send my man Storm to make the exchange. Let's say about eight-thirty this evening. It will be real busy at that time with folks buying last-minute hookups for the night."

Tastey thought about her dinner date with Tony and wanted to make the drop-off sometime tomorrow. Yet she also knew, first and foremost, she was in town for business, and Zack's worrisome-ass would bug the fuck out if she messed this exchange up. "All right then, eight-thirty. Have him sit on the bench in front of the pizza stand in the food court. Put the cash in a shopping bag. You and Zack supposed to go way back, so he says, so there's no need to count it. He trusts you!" Tastey made her words sound like a threat. Deacon had mad respect for Zack because of his successful strip club experience and would never try to dick him. Besides, where would he go? Zack's grandma knew his grandma out there in Detroit.

Ending the call, Deacon gave his boy Storm the details of his and Tastey's brief talk. Deacon put the money in the bag, like requested, and gave it to Storm. As he parted ways with them, Deacon and O.T. prayed for the best.

Storm hoped Kenya wouldn't call him until he finished taking care of his business. Taking a hot shower he got dressed for the night. Planning on taking her to dinner at Lady Fee's Place, Storm was intent on showing her a good time. It was a jazz cafe that only cats with deep pockets could afford to take their girl to. Lady Fee's only sold the whole bottles of wine, not a glass. The smallest steak was forty-five dollars and that didn't include an entire meal. That was just for a sandwich.

"This female is something special. Fuck what them busters talking about. I want her ass bad!" Storm was talking to himself as he checked the mirror before leaving his condo.

Meanwhile, across town, Kenya was thinking almost the same thing. *I hope this dude Storm be on time. The sooner I get rid of him, the sooner I can get with Tony.* She put on her lipstick and checked her hair one more time before she left the room. To make sure that they were on for later, she took Tony's number out her purse and picked up the hotel phone. "Hello, may I speak to Tony please?" Kenya was twirling the cord around, blushing as she talked.

"Hey, ma. This me." Tony saw the strange number and knew it was Kenya. He was of course overjoyed she called.

"I was just calling to see what was up. Were you still gonna spend some time with me later?" She tried to sound sexy.

He loved the way her voice purred already and his manhood was getting harder by the minute. "You know I ain't trying to let you get away from me that easily. I just need to make a couple of runs then I'll be ready. Give me to about nine-thirty and call me back, cool? We can get something to eat and check out some jazz at a little spot I know." Fingers crossed, he hoped that she would agree with his plans.

"Oh, that's cool with me. I just woke up anyhow," she automatically lied. Kenya was happy about the time he picked because she had to make a run also. "I'll be here waiting." She was lying again, but what could she do? Tell him she was a drug mule from Detroit and was going to make a transaction before they met up? With her game face on, she went downstairs and got into one of the cabs that were posted in front of the hotel. It was time for her to get into "Tastey" mode.

Storm pulled the low-key piece of shit he was driving into valet. He got out and tossed the attendant the keys. Even if he was riding foul, he wasn't gonna be walking all far from the door in his $1,000 gators. He looked like a businessman trying to return a package for his wife, or something of that nature. Anxious to get this over with, Storm sat down on the bench and checked his diamond-filled watch for the time. *This bitch, Tastey or whatever, better be on time!* He got out the slip of paper that Deacon had given him with the bitch's 1-800 cell phone number on it and had it in his hand.

Tastey entered the mall at the other end opposite from the food court. She wanted to peep out her surroundings before she met up with ol' boy. There was no way she wanted to get set up and possibly killed. All the stories she'd heard of her parents' murder jumped back into her head. As the out-of-towner tried to appear casual, Tastey cautiously approached the bench. She saw the back of the guy's head and a shopping bag beside his leg. Knowing that must've been the guy she was supposed to meet, her heart started to beat fast. When she got closer, she shockingly realized that it was, of all people, Tony. She forgot all about the drugs she was carrying and immediately got a serious attitude. Kenya ran up on him and let her bloodline-inherited rage take over.

"Damn, is this your little run? You picking up one of your little bitches from work and got me waiting?"

He was in shock. He was at a loss for words. "Where did you come from, Miss Lady? I thought you were supposed to be at the hotel waiting for me."

Storm was starting to get nervous because he knew that Tastey was due there any minute and didn't want Kenya to get the wrong idea. "Listen, Kenya, sweetheart, slow your roll. It ain't nothing like that." Liking her "fuck the world" mentality, he liked the fact that she set tripping, acting jealous. It made him know that he wasn't the only one who, crazy as it seemed, was catching feelings so soon.

"Is this your li'l bitch number? Let me call the trick and tell her that she's been fucking canceled for the evening!"

He had forgotten that he had Tastey's name and number in his hand. Kenya, feeling disrespected, like she ran the world, had gotten beside herself and snatched the paper out his hand. Furious, she hated for any nigga to try to play her.

Storm, seeing things were quickly going south, held his head down because he knew that all hell was about to break loose when she read that name. *Please don't let this chic Tastey show up right now and set ol' girl off even more, please!* he kept repeating in his mind over and over.

"Oh hell fuck naw!" Kenya rolled her eyes, shaking her head. "Ain't this some crazy shit," she hissed while sucking her teeth.

"Listen, baby. I'm trying to tell you it ain't like that. It's just business!" He was trying his best to take a cop like they'd known each other for years. "I don't even know the stankin' bitch. I swear!"

Kenya looked into his eyes and saw that he was starting to look hurt and decided to let him off the hook. "Damn, baby, why I gotta be all that? Tell Deacon he needs to teach you some manners. So, Tony, they call you Storm, huh?"

Storm stood up, giving her a dumbfounded look. "Is that why you in town? You're Tastey? Oh my God! You right! Ain't this some shit?" He had to smile too at the irony of the situation.

After about ten minutes of tripping on what they were obviously there to accomplish, the couple decided to split up and meet after they finished both their business. He walked her to the taxi stand at the mall and kissed her. This time it was a small peck on her lips.

"You know this is a sign, right? We're supposed to be together." Storm wanted her even more. He knew that she had game and would have a nigga's back in the streets if need be.

"Okay then, I'll meet you at nine-thirty in front of the hotel. And don't keep me waiting!" She blew a kiss to him as the cab pulled off away from the curb. Storm wanted to drive her back himself personally, but having drugs, a gun, and a lot of money in the car didn't mix no matter which way you calculated it.

Within minutes of Kenya getting back in her room, her cell phone rang again. "Yes, baby!" She answered it without checking the caller ID, assuming it was Storm.

"Hey, Kenya, is that you?" It was her twin sister and it sounded like she was crying.

"What's wrong, London, why you crying?" Kenya was instantly frantic, hearing her sister moan.

London started crying harder and couldn't get the words out, so Fatima took the phone out of her hand. "Hey, Kenya. This is Fatima." She focused on driving while preparing to deliver her roommate's sister the tragic family news. "Girl, you need to come home. There's been an accident. Your uncle has been shot. We're on the road now on our way to Detroit."

Kenya was full of questions, just as London was when she first heard the news. "I thought he was in jail."

Fatima was trying to drive and talk and had to cut the conversation short. "Listen, Kenya, I know you're out of town, but you need to catch the first flight back. We'll see you when you get here."

Kenya quickly packed her shit up and stashed the money in different suitcases. She checked out the hotel and rushed to the airport. There was a flight leaving in eighty-six minutes and she planned to be on it if at all possible. On the ride to the airport, she tried to call Heads Up, but didn't get an answer. It constantly went straight to voicemail. She then decided to call Storm and explain to him what she'd just heard and had jumped back home. "Hey, baby, I'm not going to be able to have dinner with you. I'm on my way to the airport."

Storm could tell that she was upset. "What happened, why?" Storm was truly interested as well as disappointed they couldn't have dinner. He turned the radio down in his car so he could give Kenya his full, undivided attention. He was really feeling Kenya. There was something special about her that he liked.

"I want to stay but I just got a call. My uncle had an accident and he's the only family I really have." Kenya was crying on the phone like her sister was doing less than thirty minutes prior.

"Listen, Kenya, I'm sorry to hear that. Have a safe flight and please promise me that you'll call me as soon as you get a chance. I wanna still take you to dinner one day even if I have to fly to Detroit to do it."

Agreeing to stay in touch, they both hung up the phone.

Chapter Sixteen

The Aftermath

FIVE DEAD AND ONE CRITICALLY INJURED was the headline in Saturday's morning edition newspaper. It was also the top story on every single television channel in Detroit. All three—Kenya, London, and Fatima—sat almost as still as mummies as they watched report after report flash across the flat screen mounted on the wall.

"This seems like a nightmare. I can't figure it out. How did all of this happen?" Bewildered, London was almost in shock as she shook her head.

Kenya's eyes were close to being swollen shut from all the tears that she had shed, and she was just as confused, losing more than one good friend in the melee.

Fatima, being supportive to the twins, went into the kitchen to get some tea for all of them. Fatima then came back in and turned the television up. It was the top of the hour and the girls were waiting to see if they could get some accurate additional information about what went down at the club that night, since the police were being so hush-hush about the details of the case.

"Good morning. I'm standing in front of Heads Up, known as a notorious popular gentlemen's club, located on the far east side of the city. This location was the backdrop for one of the most senseless, vicious, fatal shootouts in recent times in Detroit. It was inside of this very building, shortly after seven-thirty p.m., that shots rang out. Needless to say pure terror erupted. The callous gunmen fired aimlessly into the crowd, striking several people and causing injuries to others who were trampled by innocent bystanders trying to escape the line of gunfire." The newscaster was shaking his head. "On the screen we have the pictures of the deceased."

The girls' eyes continued to be glued to the screen.

"They are, Zack Carter, forty-one, the club owner, Monique Peterson, nineteen, a dancer and mother, Angela Sims, forty, the club manager, Jason Roberts, thirty-nine, who was paroled from prison just hours before the shooting, and Professor Sanford Kincade, forty-three, who taught political science at State University. Another person is listed in critical condition. He is identified as Rasul Hakim Akbar, thirty-five, who is the head of security at Heads Up."

The reporter's face looked agitated as he continued with the grim accounts of the previous evening. "For several years now people have being trying to get this strip club shut down. Now, with the owner being gunned down inside of his own establishment, some might just get their wish granted. The police are still looking for two or more gunmen. They have no motives as of yet for these murders. Anyone with information is asked to call Homicide. This is Marcus Randal, reporting for channel seven news."

"Did you see that shit?" Fatima, in the midst of the gloominess that was consuming the room, was falling over laughing.

"Oh my God, yes! I can't believe it. What was his slimy-ass doing down here?" London was still sad, shocked, and visibly shaken because of her uncle's death, but like Fatima she was also full of glee at the news report.

Kenya watched the two of them and finally blurted out, "I don't get it. Can one of you bitches fill me in, please?" Kenya was getting annoyed.

Fatima took the honor, explaining the reason for their amusement. "Kenya, Professor Sanford Kincade. That name doesn't ring a bell to you? Think about it. He teaches at our school!"

All of a sudden Kenya jumped up. "You bullshitting! I know that ain't that coward motherfucker who raped you?"

London was over being ashamed about what had happened to her and used it for her strength. "I guess it's true what they say: God really don't like ugly, does He?"

They all three had a good laugh as they continued to mourn Stone and Raven.

The twins went to their uncle's funeral. Kenya cried extra hard after listening to the entire backlog of messages that Stone left her. Sadly she realized that he was dead for trying to protect her. Ty even showed up at the services and he and Kenya made their peace. He explained to her that he was trying to get in touch with her so bad because he owed her uncle a favor. Stone had kept some guys in jail from kicking his ass and in return he promised to get his niece to answer her phone.

After seeing her uncle's picture on Zack's wall, Kenya realized they'd known one another years prior. Yet, she didn't know that Zack had also known her parents and Stone blamed him for their deaths. Kenya, feeling some sort of way, didn't attend Zack's or Old Skool's funeral services. She was pissed off at both of them for hiding their true identity from her, even though Old Skool in reality didn't find out who Kenya was until the end. Not that it would do any good or really matter who knew what and when, but it would be like a smack in her uncle's memory to go mourn them. *Fuck him and her!* she thought. *It's all good with me now anyway!* After all Kenya did have that cash that she had gotten from Storm and Deacon in the transaction. It was hers now, all $65,000.

She spent a little bit of the money on Raven's funeral service. Kenya knew that her family didn't have any income. Raven's mother was a junkie and got high every chance she got. The only good thing to come out of Raven's dancing in Heads Up was meeting Young Foy. He had really stepped up to the plate after that fateful night, and took Raven's small son, Jaylin, to live with him. Kenya gave him $5,000 to get on his feet and get a two-bedroom apartment for him and his new son. Young Foy promised her he would be dedicated and get off into his music, showing Jaylin a different way to make money. She also gave her twin $15,000 for school and put the rest in a safety deposit box.

London and Kenya, knowing it was time for a change and new beginnings, cleaned out Gran's house, putting a lot of stuff in storage. It was hard going through all of their childhood memories, but it was time to try to put the past behind them. The only things left were beds, a dresser, and an old couch.

"The last load is on the truck. Let's go!" Kenya was calling out to her twin sister. "We need to drop this stuff off at the storage trailer and get back. I have a plane to catch!"

Kenya had been talking to Storm every day on the phone since she'd left Dallas. They had truly fallen in love over the phone and Kenya was moving out there to be with him for a while to see how she liked Dallas. She hadn't even had the dick yet and she wanted him. They talked about a lot of stuff, but, for some reason, she didn't tell him she had a sister, let alone a twin. London hated drug dealers, so she chose not to bring it up, ever, but Kenya knew that forever was a long time to keep a secret, especially one as major as that was.

"Okay, sis, here I come." London was checking for any last-minute boxes that had to be stored before they left.

Fatima had gone back up to school to stay on top of PAID. Since London's speech, the night of the horrible shooting, the little organization was starting to really blow up and spread. A lot of East Coast schools were interested in starting chapters as well as the West. They wanted London to come and speak at their campuses and hopefully motivate their students to make a change and take a stand against illegal drugs and all the woes associated with them.

When the two girls reached the storage bin, London pulled out her set of keys and opened it, so that the guys they had hired could load it up. Kenya, trying her best to avoid any further work, went to the front desk to pay the bill up for an entire year.

"Yes, I'm here to pay the bill on bin 316." Kenya kept checking her watch. She didn't want to miss her flight.

The desk clerk got out his folder. "Yes, are you London Roberts?"

"No, I'm her sister Kenya. She's around back with the movers. I just want to pay the rental fee up for the year."

The man was happy to hear that and gave her the computer receipt. "Please sign the account holder's name."

Kenya signed London's name and put her copy of the receipt in her purse. With that exchange she was out the door.

"I'm gonna miss you so much. I love you." London was starting to cry as her sister was about to board the plane to start a new life in a new place.

"You know I'm gonna miss you too. We all we got. I'm not gonna forget that, London, even in Texas." Kenya hugged her twin tightly.

"I'm proud of you, Kenya. I always have been even though I might not say it much. You're strong and I've always envied and wanted to have that quality."

Kenya had tears streaming down her face. She was the one always proud of London.

"Give 'em hell out there, Ms. Roberts!" London smiled as Kenya boarded the plane.

Chapter Seventeen

Kenya

"All right, fellas. I gotta be out. My girl is flying in today and I don't want to be late." Storm was excited as hell that Kenya was finally on her way back to him.

"Take your henpecked-ass on then, nigga!" O.T. was still bent down, rolling the dice as he talked shit to his brother. Deacon and the rest of the guys who were in the back of the Alley Cats shooting dice laughed at O.T., who was clowning as usual.

Storm didn't give a fuck. Nothing could knock him off his square today.

By the time he stopped to pick up some roses and get his car detailed, it was time to pick Kenya up. Storm got inside the terminal hoping to see her face. She looked more gorgeous than he remembered. She had on the suit that he bought her and some sling-back pumps to match. Her hair was hanging down across her shoulders. Kenya, excited as well, ran into his open arms.

"Hey, daddy, I missed you." She closed her eyes as the two kissed for the very first time. Storm held her close and stuck his tongue in her mouth. She felt her legs getting weak.

"I missed you too, baby." They both were elated as they went to get her luggage.

"I think we gonna need something like a buggy. I've got eight bags. They made me pay extra for all that shit." Kenya was going on and on.

Storm couldn't do anything but smile. He was happy that she had a lot of bags. It showed that she really was gonna stay with him and try to make what started off as their long-distance relationship work. "You could have a hundred bags and it wouldn't matter. I'm just glad to have you here—with me."

Storm had to pay a taxi van to carry all of Kenya's bags to his condo, which was not a problem. When they pulled up, Storm gave her the keys and pointed out the door. "Go ahead and open the door up, sweetheart. I'm gonna help my man with these bags."

Kenya opened the door to her new life and stepped inside. It smelled just like jasmine and wildflowers. The living room had a huge plasma screen, a few big throw pillows on the floor, and a plant that looked like it hadn't been watered in months. She went toward the kitchen and saw that it was clean. Everything was in its place. It had a long marble countertop and the dining room had a card table and two chairs in it. Before she could go upstairs, Storm stopped her.

"Hey, we got all the bags in the front hall! I know it's empty down here, but up 'til now it's just been me. After you get settled in, you can go get living room and dining room furniture. We probably need new dishes, pots, pans, towels, and whatever else you want or think we need. How about you just make this condo all about you? I want you to be happy. This is our home now. It just needs a woman's touch."

They started to kiss again. Only this time it was much more intense than at the airport. Kenya could feel Storm's dick getting harder.

"Hold up, baby, I want our first time to be special. I want to take you to that dinner that I promised you. I want you to know that I love you and always will."

"I love you too, Storm."

They went out to dinner at Lady Fee's Place, just like he had planned months ago. Tonight would be the night that they had both dreamed of. Any- and everything on the menu was being showcased to the young couple in love. After devouring a fantastic meal, Storm and Kenya were soon almost finished with their desserts. The two had drunk almost the entire bottle of wine as they ate their meals and talked. Kenya took her shoe off, seductively running her foot along the side of his leg. Storm's eyes grew wide when Kenya finally reached the hardness in between his legs.

"Baby, you know you wrong for doing this to a brother out in public."

Kenya smiled and continued rubbing his manhood with her foot until she felt it damn near ready to bust out through his zipper.

The waitress came to the table, asking the pair of soon-to-be lovers if they needed anything else. Storm, feeling self-conscious, had to readjust himself in the seat so that she wouldn't notice the bulge in his pants. "No, thank you, just bring the bill. We're both about ready." He paid the bill, then left her a nice, fat tip and they were out the door.

"I'm glad to see you act like you have some class and tip like you're supposed to. I hate when guys don't tip."

Storm held her close and whispered in her ear. "Don't worry about that shit anymore. You're with me now. You're my girl. That means you want for nothing!"

As they made their way home they couldn't keep their hands off each other. From the time they made it through the condo door, it was on. Storm grabbed Kenya and covered her mouth with his. His tongue was moving in and out fast and deep. She held her head back as he seemed to devour her entire neck with light nibbles that were sure to leave passion marks. Storm's hands were exploring her body. Kenya, lightheaded and dizzy, felt his hands roam across her breasts and then squeeze her shoulders, never once removing his tongue from her skin. His dick was rock hard and Kenya could feel it throbbing through his pants as he pressed her body hard against the wall.

"Do you know how bad I want you? Do you understand just how much I need you?"

She could feel his hot breath in her ear as he started to caress her skin softly, sending chills throughout her whole body. A single tear started to fall from Kenya's eye and Storm quickly kissed it off of her face. He kissed both her closed eyes, the tip of her nose and called out her name, both quiet and loud at the same time.

"Let me make love to you." He took his hand and raised her face to meet his. "Feel this." Storm placed her hands on his shaft and made her fingers squeeze his dick as if she was massaging it. "This is yours, tonight, tomorrow, and forever. Let me give it to you."

Kenya could barely catch her breath. Her mind was confused. She had been fucked before, but not once had a man made love to her. The room was spinning and wouldn't slow down. Storm, with the strength of a bull, carried her up the stairs and into the bedroom. It was the only furnished room in the condo, but it was done up right. Not missing a beat, he laid her trembling body across the king-sized bed and started to undress her slowly. Storm, eager to make her totally his, kept his eyes glued on her. It would finally be time for Kenya to be the prey instead of the predator. Storm had gotten her down to her thong and a matching white lace camisole and finally felt the need to speak.

"Damn, baby, you look good as a motherfucker. I gotta have you—forever."

Kenya watched his every move as he took his belt loose and unzipped his pants. When they dropped to the plush carpet beneath him, she could see his big black dick standing at attention, curving to the side. Kenya tried to resist, but couldn't help herself as she crawled over to the edge of the bed where he was standing, and let her mouth take his dick inside. Storm moaned from pleasure as she took control of him. He heard the sweetest sounds known to man as she slurped and sucked him hard.

Storm instinctively grabbed a handful of Kenya's long hair and twisted it in between his fingers. The head of his pole was pounding. He could feel it easing its way down her throat. As if a porno king state of mind took over, he started fucking her in her mouth hard, so hard that he had to slow down and control himself before he came. Kenya, not complaining about his sudden rough demeanor, was moaning as much as Storm was. He didn't want to cum in her mouth, so he pulled back and took her hands in his. Slowly he pushed her back onto the bed and tore her thongs off, tossing them over his shoulder. Storm went to work and her pussy was full of his tongue. She was filled with love and tried to wiggle free from the grip he had on her hips, but that, of course, only gave him more pleasure.

"Let daddy give you your present!" Storm got on top of her and slowly slid his love inside of her. It filled Kenya's moist, waiting box, hitting all her walls, tickling each spot. Kenya closed her eyes as he made love to and fucked the shit out of her at the same time.

They made love most of the night until they both fell asleep. When they woke up the next morning, it was on again—round two.

Ticktock

It had been a few months since Kenya and Storm began their new lives together. She'd just finished remodeling the condo the way that she wanted it. She had a lot of new friends and was happier than she had ever been in her life. Since Storm and his brother O.T. were so close and always together, it made her and O.T.'s on-again off-again girlfriend, Paris, kinda cool. They would go shopping and talk shit about the fellas for hours on end. Paris and Kenya were both fly as hell and didn't take any shit from either one of the brothers. They put one another up on any bullshit that the two siblings would try to pull, especially O.T. And truth be told, Paris was the only one that O.T., a straight-up fool, would halfway listen to.

Kenya really liked her new job. Storm got his boy Deacon to let her manage the bar. In reality, she was doing him a favor. She had a lot of strip club experience from dancing at Heads Up, not to mention the fact that she knew how to balance the books. Zack had taught her that much. She knew that one day it would come in handy and it did. Kenya even had all the girls in check, making money and not focused on silly bullshit that could and would occur when a gang of females got tighter under one roof. Storm was always impressed at Kenya's people skills, as well as Deacon, who knew she was trained by Zack, once his hero in the nightclub business. Alley Cats was now the new blazing hot spot in Dallas just as Heads Up was in Detroit. From NBA players, musicians, and doctors, to the average nine-to-five guy from down the block around the way, they all came to hang out at the club, have a great time, and, most importantly to the bottom line, spend money. Dudes and females alike would party inside together with few incidents. They had a slamming menu and the most exotic-looking dancers in the entire city on deck nightly.

Deacon and Storm were both making money hand over fist. They agreed that after six more months of slinging dope, they would retire from the game and open another club, go legal. They had a new supply pipeline from across the border and were getting their product at a bargain price. The more they would buy, the sweeter the deal was. However, Deacon and Storm weren't the only crew that was getting money in the city. A yesteryear player, Royce, and a couple of other older guys had been doing their thing for years across town. They were more laidback than Storm and Deacon, but stayed in their lanes unless it was necessary for them all to cross paths.

Royce

"Hey, Deacon, did you read today's paper?" Storm came in the club with the newspaper tucked under his arm.

Deacon was pissed. "Yeah, I read that bullshit! We gotta slow this shit the fuck down. The cops are running up in all the houses that are on the north side. It's getting wild out there like it's an election year or something!"

Storm poured himself a shot of Remy. "Yeah, I feel you. We need to try to sit down with that old, wrinkled nigga Royce and figure some shit out that can help us all. I know that he gots to be hurting just as much as we are, shit, probably even more."

Deacon knew his partner was right. He had an idea that might smooth things out for both crews. "You know what, I'll send one of the girls over to the spot where Royce and his crew hangs out at, and ask him to come to the club for dinner, drinks, and discussion. We gotta slow these motherfucking police raids the fuck down! This shit gotta stop!"

It was Thursday night when Royce and three of his main men decided to take Deacon and Storm up on their invitation for a sit-down. They were all suited and booted acting as if they were going to a funeral or some cornball shit-bag-ass job. That's how Royce and his boys rolled every day everywhere they went. Most of his crew were younger and rarely dressed like their boss, but some were desperate to fit in and possibly raise in the ranks, so they followed his lead, dressing like men three times their age.

"Look at these old players, players who done escape from the museum." Storm nodded in the direction of the door and Deacon glanced over to see what his boy was talking about.

"Well, baby boy. Let's do this shit!" Deacon patted Storm on his shoulder, reassuring him that his idea to meet with Royce would have a good outcome. When they started to walk over to the table, Storm stopped one of the shot girls and asked her to bring over a bottle of Hennessy VSOP and several glasses for the special guests.

After all the talking and trying to peep each other out, the two rival crews had come to an agreement. Both of them hardcore, not wanting to be the first to blink, were reluctant to give any sort of solid guarantee, but would try to stop any more unnecessarily outrageous violence in their zones. It would be hard to promise a 100 percent total truce, because they were at war. And with war, there were always casualties. That was a given. But for now, the police and the everyday snitches were common enemies they could beef with together as a unit.

"Why don't you gentlemen enjoy the rest of your evening? Of course, everything is compliments of Alley Cats." Deacon then called a waitress over, authorizing her to put everything on his book. "Tell the girls to take care of my friends here. I'm going to take care of their fee. Dances on me!"

Royce stood up to shake both Deacon's and Storm's hands. "Listen, young brothers. I respect both of you as men, and I wish you well. You try to handle your end and I got mine. Thanks for the hospitality. My crew and myself appreciate it to the fullest."

For a Thursday night, the bar was off the hook. Kenya had booked a featured dancer from back east, who was also an XXX porn star. Cum4u was on stage performing the most erotic, nasty, and shocking dance routine ever seen to man or beast. She'd not only captured every one of the males' attention, but the other dancers, the wait staff, and Kenya, who thought that she had seen it all; but this ho was a master at the craft of entertaining a crowd. She was bending like a pretzel and licking every part of her own body. The crowd loved it as they watched, spellbound.

"Damn, Kenya! Where in the hell you get her from?" Deacon was also amazed as he lusted for the flexible young dancer on stage. "That ho wifey material!"

"Come on now, you know a chic like me got skills and contacts. Look around. Everyone is buying drinks and spending money. I'm about that life." Kenya was doing her thang and knew it.

Deacon patted Storm on his back while looking at Kenya. "Damn, girl, tell me you have a sister, a cousin, even a close friend anything like you. You know how to make shit really happen. Plus you fine as hell!" They opened a bottle of Moët and toasted to the club and making money for the rest of their young lives.

"Just like me?" Kenya laughed out loud to her inside joke. "Naw, sorry, Deacon. I'm an original, besides, what the fuck would y'all do with two of me running around?"

Deacon, Storm, and Kenya were finishing up the bottle when Royce and his crew, done taking advantage of Deacon and Storm's offer of hospitality, were leaving, heading toward the door. Royce, old but not blind, couldn't help but stare lustfully at Kenya. Alley Cats had some bad bitches swinging from poles and grinding in laps on the payroll, but Kenya was the finest of them all, and she had all of her clothes on.

"Damn, fellas, where did you have this one hiding at all night? She the real showstopper!" Royce was looking her up and down, from foot to fro, licking his lips, imagining what he'd do to her given the opportunity.

Making sure Royce knew what was really good, Storm wrapped his arms around Kenya's small waist. "Hold tight, this here is top shelf, cat daddy! This all me!" He started kissing her on the neck while Royce marveled at the young man's eye candy.

"Damn, I can respect that. Let me just say, you're one lucky man." Royce envied him as he grinned.

As Royce and his crew left out the door, Deacon and Storm were overly amused at his game, or lack of it.

"Old players kill me. They just don't know when their time in the sun is over! Shit, it's our time to shine bright!" Storm gave Deacon a dap and they continued drinking the rest of the night.

Chapter Eighteen

London

Within the few months of London returning to school, a lot of things had changed. The first thing being that PAID had blown up far beyond her dreams. The days following the big meeting she'd spoken at got a lot of people motivated. Both students and politicians alike were starting to get involved in the newly formed movement. Not only was her campus fired up, so were schools all across the East Coast. Different schools were forming chapters of PAID and were getting London to speak on their campus.

"Wow, I never thought we would be getting this much mail!" Fatima was going through all the correspondence that the organization was receiving.

"Girl, I know what you're saying. This entire thing has us so busy, it's getting hard for me to study. I need some sort of a break."

Fatima smirked as she spoke. "Well, stop getting folks so damned geeked up with your speeches and maybe you can get some rest."

London sat back on her bed, wondering what her twin was up to. It had been more than a hot minute since the two had talked on the phone and she missed at least hearing her voice if nothing else. She hoped that Kenya's new life was everything that she wanted it to be and more, but still secretly prayed for her to move back home. London tried calling Kenya a couple of times, but her cell phone always went straight to voicemail. She knew her sister and knew Kenya would get back to her in her own time.

Fatima, who'd been acting somewhat peculiar since the night of the shooting at Heads Up, was looking in the mirror, fixing her hair. Strangely, she'd been making a lot of trips to Detroit over the last few months for reasons London couldn't quite figure out or put her finger on. "Hey, girl, I have to make a short trip to your city. Do you want to roll with me so you can check on the house or visit some of your old neighbors or friends? For real, not trying to get off into your business, but you and Kenya should accept one of those offers and close that chapter in your life so you can start a new one." Fatima, outta nothing but love, was always concerned about her roommate's well-being.

"Naw, girl, I'm tight on all that travel. I think I'm gonna just try to fall back, get some rest, and study this weekend. Besides, I know how you like dumping me off somewhere in the city while you take care of your secret stuff you got going on." London playfully pushed her roommate's shoulder, teasing.

"Stop playing. You know I don't have any secrets I'm hiding from you, soul sista. I'm just doing some volunteer work, that's all."

"Yeah, right, stop it! Way in Detroit?" Fatima and London giggled and talked about a lot of different stuff before the two went to sleep.

Morning came and Fatima was up, dressed, and ready to hit the highway early. "Are you sure you don't want to ride?"

London was sitting on the side of her bed, rubbing her eyes. "Girl, go do you. I think I should read a few more of these letters from other schools and respond. There's even a few from out on the West Coast trying to organize. This thing is a monster!"

With an exchange of hugs, Fatima hit the road while London started to read and reply to the letters by e-mail.

Storm

Storm was pissed the fuck off. He never really got upset but when money was involved he turned into a pure maniac. "Son of a bitch! When is this bullshit gonna cease? My pockets are starting to feel this shit. For real, for real I'm over it!"

Storm and Deacon were getting a lot of complaints from their workers on the block. It seemed as if a lot of do-right organizations were starting to form all along the West Coast hell-bent on slowing down if not attempting to stop altogether the sale of drugs in certain low-income areas.

Deacon was heated as well as he cracked his knuckles. "I know that nigga Royce is pissed off too. I saw him and his boys out at the mall and he was complaining about getting his hard."

Storm and his brother O.T. were shooting pool and trying to come up with a new game plan as Deacon paced the floor, almost wearing a hole in the carpet. After about an hour or so, they decided to set up another meeting with Royce. They knew he got all his dope from the same connect as they did, an old man in the Islands named Javier. If both crews could hopefully arrange a sit-down with the "elusive of the law" kingpin, maybe they could slightly lower the ticket and be able to stay above board until the heat of whatever was taking place would slow down and it could be back to business as usual.

"Real talk, I'm gonna call his phone and see if he wants to bump heads on this shit." Deacon went to get the number and make the call. "I know he sick right now just like we is!"

"Yeah, do that, while I finish tapping your boy's ass on this table." O.T. laughed as he put chalk on his cue. "Ain't gonna be nothing nice, son, know that!"

Deacon soon came out of the office with a big smile on his grill. "I talked to Royce. We're gonna meet at the football game two weeks from now. He said he got some tickets reserved for all of us." Storm gave Deacon a stupid look and O.T. took over from there.

"It better not be any damn nosebleed seats up high. You know them old motherfuckers are broke as a fuck."

"Man, shut your young-ass up!" Deacon was shaking his head, laughing at his comments.

O.T. continued to clown, having such an easy target to talk shit about. "I ain't playing. That ancient Negro gonna make me catch a case up in that bitch if them seats is foul. That's my word! Don't nobody wanna be sitting damn near in heaven watching the game with the angels!"

By that time Storm was falling out too, holding his side. "Man, I'm out. I gotta get to the crib. Kenya is cooking dinner and I don't want to be late." Storm grabbed his jacket and headed toward the door.

"Yo, give her a kiss for me." Deacon gave Storm some love and went over to the pool table to give O.T. a much-needed lesson in losing.

Kenya

Storm and Kenya were sitting down at the table and finishing up the meal she'd prepared for them.

"Damn, baby, that shit was on point. You've got the total package, beauty, brains, and you can cook like a motherfucker. How did I get so lucky?"

Kenya cleared the table off and poured each of them another glass of wine. "I love you so much, Storm. I swear, you're my entire world." She went and sat on his lap, resting her head on his chest. "When you gonna marry me?" As soon as the words came out of Kenya's mouth, she couldn't believe that she had said that shit. She had a look of embarrassment on her face. They hadn't been together a year, but it didn't matter, she was all in.

"Baby, let me take care of a few projects and I plan on doing just that, make you my wife. I want to make sure that I can buy us a house first."

Storm asked Kenya if she would go in the floor safe in the guest bedroom and bring all the money down. He wanted to get an accurate count and see just what he was working with as far as cash on hand. Kenya had been putting his money in the safe both from the streets and his cut from the club almost nightly. He let her handle the cash because she was good at balancing shit.

"Baby, this money is our future." Storm spread all the money on the floor and started to count.

While he was doing that, Kenya decided to check her messages from her cell phone. It said that she had seventeen new calls. After checking each one, she went upstairs to call London. It had been months and Storm still didn't know that she had an identical twin sister living back in Detroit. Maybe it was London's strong opposition to drugs: the one main thing that paid her and Storm's bills and would ultimately pay for their new house. Whatever her reason was, Kenya felt the strong need not to tell him—at least, not yet.

"Hey, girl, I missed you." Kenya shut the door behind her for some added privacy.

"I missed you too. I've been trying to call you ever since last week. We got a good offer on the house and I want to take it." London was ready to let go and move on just as Fatima had suggested. "What do you think? Unless there's a chance you might move back home!"

"All right, London, you set up the meeting with the real estate agent and I'll catch a flight out there. Just give me a couple of weeks. I seriously don't think I'll be moving back and if I do, I wouldn't want to stay in that neighborhood."

Sad to hear Kenya's final verdict about relocating back to Detroit, the twins chatted a little bit more about all the hell that London was causing on the entire East Coast and of course how Kenya's new life was going in Dallas. When they hung up the phone Kenya made her way back downstairs. Storm was almost done counting all the cash and asked Kenya to run him some bathwater. When the water was just right, they both got in the tub and before even five minutes had past, they were making love. Storm's strong hands were firmly gripping Kenya's waist as her body took on a total sense of relaxation and pleasure. He pulled her wet hair as he slowly eased in and out of her. After repeating the calculated stroke motions over and over, Storm and Kenya both moaned out in passion as they started to climax together.

The two of them remained embraced in the water, talking until the water grew cold. Storm got out first and brought his woman a huge white fluffy towel. He picked her up out the tub and wrapped her up like a baby. Storm then carried her back to their bed and slowly started drying her off.

"Do you know how much I love you? You're my queen!" Storm kissed her hands and started sucking her fingers one by one.

Kenya was on cloud nine and confused. Anytime Storm touched her, she still trembled. She closed her eyes trying to stay focused. Kenya had to think of a lie and fast. She finally told him that she had to fly back east in a few weeks for her godson's birthday. Anytime she mentioned him, Storm would melt just as she did. He truly loved

Kenya for her loyalty to the little boy despite not being blood related. She hated lying to her man, but what else could she do? Tell him her twin dope-dealer-hating sister and her had business to tend to?

Chapter Nineteen

Storm

As always, time flew by and Storm, Deacon, and O.T. went to meet with Royce at the football game. Just as O.T. feared the seats were terrible. Also, just as equally as they were feeling the pain of the new antidrug movements being formed on the West Coast, so was Royce. Most of the conversation was filled with different angles that they could use to push their products and gain more revenue. All parties involved felt that selling dope was a game to be run and operated like a Wall Street firm. They had strict rules to follow and sometimes a guy had to check his ego at the door if he planned on being profitable.

Although the two crews were rivals in Dallas, they both understood that it would be advisable for them to join forces with one another, cooperate, and try to set up a face-to-face with Javier. Both of the crews' pockets were suffering and at that present point in time neither wanted to relocate their business dealings in an attempt to start all over again, possibly ending up with the same headache. The two rivals joining forces could be the final deal-breaker in coming up or the final nail in their coffins, much depending on Javier's answer.

Royce and Deacon jointly made the conference call to Mexico, making the travel arrangements with a reserved but open-minded Javier. If things went as planned, all the parties involved could get back to business as usual—making money.

Kenya

"Baby, you know that I'm gonna miss you while you're gone. I wish that I could fly out east with you and meet your godson." Storm was covering Kenya's face with kisses. He loved her with all his inner being. It was the first time that he truly opened his heart up to a woman. She was the one he'd waited for his whole life. He felt like the sun would rise and set on Kenya.

"I love you, daddy! You know I'm gonna miss you too, you and this dick." Kenya started to rub on his pants and his manhood instantly jumped to attention.

Storm held Kenya tightly in his arms and hugged her like there was no tomorrow in sight. "Before you get on that plane and fly away from me, I want you to take this with you and promise me that you're gonna come back to me!" Storm reached in his pocket, pulling out an engagement ring and slipped it on to Kenya's finger. "Will you marry me?"

The room grew silent as Kenya stood in shock, weak in the knees.

"Well, is that silence a yes or a no?"

"Yes! Yes! Yes!" Kenya, ecstatic, jumped up and down.

Storm and Kenya made love in the middle of the floor until it was time for him to take her to the airport. Kenya felt guilty for lying to the man she loved about her secret life back in Detroit. Admiring the ring he'd just placed on her finger, she made a promise to herself that when she got back to Dallas she would tell him the truth about everything she'd been hiding, especially London, and let the chips fall where they may. She prayed their love was strong enough to overcome whatever.

Storm

Storm had just returned from dropping his new wife-to-be off and had to get ready to meet Deacon at the club. He, Deacon, and Royce were flying out in the afternoon. The meeting with Javier was set and they hoped that it would go well. O.T. was going to stay behind and run things at the Alley Cats until Storm and Deacon returned. It was going to be a few days of terror at the club, because O.T. was a straight-up fool and everyone on staff knew it. Deacon had to leave a detailed list of do's and don'ts for him to follow. He was a clown, but with Kenya out east, unfortunately he was the next in line to run the place.

"Damn, it's getting about that time." Storm looked at his watch. Kenya had packed his bag for him and had everything neat as hell. Storm looked at the picture of both of them on the dresser and threw it in his bag for good luck. He missed her smile already. *I just need to put this cash up. Damn, why didn't I remember to get Kenya to put it in the safe before she left?*

He went to the guest bedroom and went into the closet. After moving all the clothes and boxes that Kenya had stacked up over the floor safe, he opened it, tossing the money inside. As he started to throw all the stuff back like he'd found it, a box fell down, almost hitting him in the head. The contents were scattered across the floor. It was a gang of papers that obviously belonged to Kenya. They were mostly old bills and receipts from what he could tell. Without paying much attention, he stuffed them back into the box, until one of them stood out.

"Motown Storage Units" was on the top of one of the paper printouts. It was dated the day that Kenya had flown out to be with him. He knew that she had a few things still out there that she couldn't bring on the plane, so that wasn't the big problem. The problem was the signature on the receipt. *Who in the hell is London Roberts?* He had seen Kenya's ID when they signed some insurance papers. He recognized Kenya's handwriting. He knew Amoya Kenya Roberts was her government name for certain, but who was London Roberts and how was she related to Kenya? Time was flying and he had to go pick up Deacon so they could catch their flight. He put the paper in his wallet and would ask Kenya about it when she got home or the next time they spoke. He trusted Kenya and knew that there was a good explanation for it.

Storm arrived at Alley Cats just as Deacon was giving O.T. the rundown on things and last-minute instructions as to how he wanted things done in his absence. Deacon and Storm were only going to be gone two or three days tops, but a lot of shit could happen between then and now, especially with O.T. running things. After they were totally convinced that O.T. had it down, they headed to the airport. Storm darted in and out of traffic and they made it to the terminal in record time.

"Damn, I was just out here. I should have just stayed out here, had a couple of drinks, and met you at the gate." Storm and Deacon walked past the terminal that Kenya's plane had just departed from.

"Man, when is Kenya coming back?" Deacon wished that she had never left. Leaving O.T. at the helm made him a nervous wreck. That club was his whole life and he knew Storm's little brother could run it into the ground almost overnight.

"Relax, guy. She should be back in a few days. Just chill, ol' boy got you."

After a minute or two they saw Royce and his boy turn the corner. They had their suits on and looked like some played-out car salesmen desperate for a deal. Deacon told

Storm that this was sure to be the longest trip in history. Storm just laughed, knowing his best friend was about right this time even though he was busy missing Kenya. Royce and his boy greeted the two of them and waited for their plane to be ready to board.

"Where is that fine-ass woman you always have on your arm?" Royce questioned Storm, referring to Kenya.

"She had to fly out east to take care of some business. Plus she's not just my woman, she's my soon-to-be wife!"

Royce, his boy, and even Deacon all looked shocked at his announcement. They all congratulated him and jokingly told him to make sure to turn in his player's card before he got home.

The flight was a little bumpy, but it wasn't that long before they landed. A luxury car met them at the obscure airport and drove them all to a private airstrip at the edge of town. There they got on a smaller jet and finally reached Javier's exclusive villa. It was like a small paradise inside of a paradise. All of the small-time hustlers, compared to Javier's apparent wealth status, were impressed. When they got inside, a small-framed woman showed them to their individual deluxe suites. Each one was decorated with items that were obviously worth more than they ever hoped to afford in several lifetimes. With a welcoming spirit, she gave them fresh towels and informed them that Mr. Javier wanted them to relax, enjoy, and partake in his home's vast amenities, and he would meet with them the next day.

The Twins

Kenya's plane landed on schedule and London and Fatima were both there to meet her.

"Hey, girl, I missed your ass!" Kenya was screaming as she hugged her sister.

"I missed you too. Look at you, still looking all fly as always." London was also elated to see her twin. Fatima had to practically pry the two apart so that she could get a hug from Kenya. They gossiped and giggled all the way back to the hotel where Kenya was staying.

"We have the meeting with the real estate agent set up for the morning. Can you please wake up and get ready by ten a.m.?" London smiled as she messed with her sister. "I know how you do!"

"Yeah, yeah, yeah, girl, I can make it up by then, I guess. My husband-to-be gets up early and runs a few miles every day and I make him breakfast!" Kenya leaned back in the seat, waiting for a response.

"What do you mean, husband-to-be?" London did a double take at her twin sister, raising one eyebrow. She and Fatima were in shock as Kenya waved around the big rock on her finger that they had failed to notice. "Oh my God! When did all this happen? When am I going to meet him?" London was full of questions as she examined the size of the center stone.

"Don't worry, when I get back home I'm going to set something up, I promise."

Fatima had to go on one of her famous top-secret missions and then make a trip up to the school, so she left the sisters alone. The twins sat up all night talking and having fun. They missed each other and by the way they carried on it showed. The conversation started on Storm and the new life Kenya was leading, to London and her organization spreading across the United States.

"Girl, you are going to love Storm. He treats me like gold. It's just like being a little kid in a candy store. Whatever I want or dream about, he makes possible." Kenya was going on and on about her happiness.

"I'm so very glad for you both. As soon as this semester is complete, I'm going to visit, if that's okay. He sounds wonderful. What does he do for a living?" London quizzed her twin, trying to gain more information about the man who had her sister so wide open.

Kenya wasn't prepared for any of London's often judgmental statements, so she quickly flipped the script, changing the subject. Of course, Kenya was the queen of manipulation. It worked and the two were soon discussing London and her love life or lack of it. The back-and-forth conversation went on for hours.

The Meeting

It was a bright, sunny morning on the private island. Storm regretted that he didn't have the love of his life, Kenya, to share the gorgeous sunrise with him. As he got dressed, he looked a picture of them that he had thrown in his bag, and as corny as it seemed he kissed it.

Storm and Deacon got to the patio just as Royce and his boy did. It was 10:00 in the morning, on a tropical island, and Royce was still wearing a suit, even though it was damn near a hundred degrees in the shade.

"That nigga gonna rock that suit bullshit to the end!" Deacon laughed as he drank a glass of juice. "That hot-ass fabric is a damn heatstroke waiting to happen!"

Storm, like all the other invited guests, was sitting back thinking about what it would be like to be as rich and prosperous as Javier. Just then, two huge men entered the area. A matter of seconds later a short, balding old man joined them. Although none of the men had actually met their host, they could tell from the amount of respect shown by the staff that this was indeed the infamous Javier. He soon introduced himself and removed all doubt of his identity. He poured himself a glass of juice and then began to speak.

"I am, as some may say, a man of few words. Let me start by saying that I do appreciate you all coming to me like men to try to find a solution to your problems, and not trying to locate another supplier. I already know what your main obstacle is, and I have already put one of my best men on top of it. His name is Swift and he is already in the States. He will be sure to make all your problems go, should we say, away. I believe in cutting the monster's head off and that's what Swift will most certainly do. My people are passing around a picture of the source for you to see the face of the so-called Big Bad Wolf who's causing you such a great loss of money and grief. A silly little girl!"

Royce got the picture first and stared at it long and hard. His eyes were almost jumping out of his head. He leaped out of his seat and asked Javier if he could see him in private.

"Please, sir, I mean you no disrespect, but this is urgent!" Royce looked as if like he had seen a ghost.

Javier remained calm as he spoke. "Mr. Royce, we have no secrets here around this table. Feel free to speak your mind, no harm will come to the righteous, I can assure you of that!" Javier stared intensely at Royce, who was turning paler by the seconds. Storm and Deacon were watching him also.

Royce finally spoke. "I think these two are undercover police or something!"

Deacon and Storm both jumped out of their seats and couldn't believe what Royce had just blurted out alleging. "Man, what in the fuck are you talking about?" Storm, immediately infuriated and insulted, barked. "Are you fucking crazy, old man?"

"I'm talking about this bitch right here! Your woman is out east now ain't she? I mean that is what you told me!" Royce threw the picture across the table at Storm, who picked it up and started shaking his head, confused, in disbelief. Royce then started calling Storm a fucking snitch-ass rat who couldn't be trusted.

Javier sat back and watched the heated exchange take place among the three men. He told Royce and his boy to give him some time to sort this unfortunate mess out. Royce was asked to enjoy the rest of the day on the island relaxing and that he soon would be rewarded for his loyalty. After carefully observing Storm's and Deacon's responses to seeing the picture, he then reacted when dealing with them. Showing his power, the old man waved his hand and had his men remove both Storm and Deacon from the table and lead them to a back room.

Storm was totally speechless and in shock. He couldn't understand what he had just seen.

Deacon was terrified. "Damn, man, what the fuck is Kenya off into? I knew that bitch was too fucking good to be true. I can't believe this shit! What did she say she was flying out east for anyway?" He asked Storm question after question, knowing their lives were on the line.

"Listen, Deacon, I swear to you, guy, I don't know what the fuck is going on. Maybe these old cats are trying to test us or something? Besides, it was your boy Zack who turned us on to her in the first place. So stop pointing fucking fingers at me, okay?"

They were confused as hell and scared of what the outcome might be if this tangled web of deception wasn't straightened out fast. The two friends paced the floor as they tried to think of an explanation for the shit they were now in. After about an hour or so of being locked in the room, they heard footsteps approaching. They both started to sweat, as they watched the doorknob start to turn. The door was swung wide open and a group of men rushed inside, followed by a slow-paced Javier. As he entered the room, he focused all of his attention on to Storm. He had the picture of Kenya and Storm dangling from his hand. Javier had his men search Storm's luggage for any clues or evidence linking them to the mystery woman in the picture and what Royce had claimed to be true. They easily discovered the picture, along with a piece of paper, in his wallet.

"Okay, you men have your orders." Javier gave his crew a slight nod. Some of his men grabbed Deacon by his throat, dragging him out of the room. He was begging for his life as he struggled to breathe. His eyes were bulging out his head. "Don't beg! It shows no pride. Be a man," was all that Javier said in a nonchalant manner while still watching Storm, who two other men were holding back. Deacon didn't take Javier's advice and could be heard screaming as they took him in the basement. Javier seemed cold and unbothered about what was obviously about to take place. Deacon was undoubtedly on his way to heaven or hell thanks to an awful misunderstanding.

"Please, Javier! I don't know what's going on. I swear to God!" Storm was panicking, wanting the men to release Deacon before it was too late. "Listen, I know it looks bad, but it's not like that. That female in the picture can't be my girl. It doesn't make any kind of sense. My woman is down for me. She loves me! Something ain't right! She ain't no damn police! Trust me, she's not!"

Javier's men threw Storm in a chair and tied him up. He was still trying to explain, even though he didn't understand himself. Even though he was facing death, he couldn't grasp why or how his beloved Kenya could betray him like it seemed like she'd done. "It's not her! It must be a mistake! Let me call her! She can explain!"

"Please don't play with my intelligence, young man. The way you looked at that picture was a dead giveaway of your guilt and if I wanted more proof, you yourself provided it to me. So please stop with the lies." Javier held the picture of Storm and Kenya up next to the picture that he'd passed around earlier at the table. As he lit a cigar, he asked Storm once again, "Do you care to try to explain?" Storm just shook his head and looked toward the ground. "I didn't think so," Javier mocked, blowing smoke rings in the air.

Storm was in shock. The girl in the picture looked just like Kenya, only without makeup. How could this be? Storm was lost in his thoughts. How could this be his Kenya, but how could it not be? The final nail in the coffin came as Javier held up the paper that he had gotten out of Storm's wallet. He read the words that headlined the page. It said "Motown Storage Units." It was the same receipt that Storm found in the closet and wanted to ask Kenya about himself.

Javier read off the name that was at the bottom of the page. Storm heard the name and couldn't believe what he heard. His mouth dropped open, remembering the name also. "I guess that you still don't know who London Roberts is, do you?"

Storm was heartbroken. Not because he knew he was about to die, but because he believed that Kenya had betrayed him. Javier motioned for his men to take Storm away. They untied Storm and snatched him up from the chair. Unlike Deacon, he didn't scream, fight, or negotiate as he was led away to the unknown. Javier and his men couldn't hurt him any worse than he believed that his once-cherished Kenya had already done

Chapter Twenty

The Twins

It was 10:30 in the morning and the twins had just come back from signing the final papers on the sale of the house. They both cried at the real estate office, but knew that it was time to move on. It would take some time for the people to close on the house and the girls were happy. It gave them time to sleep at the house a few more nights, just for old time's sake. Although the pair had most of their belongings in storage, they still had their old beds there. The girls knew that they wouldn't have any use for twin beds in their new future endeavors. They were both grown and leading different lives. As soon as the two entered the house, they felt a sense of calm. It was almost as if Gran was watching over them, telling them it was okay and she approved of what they'd done.

Hearing a car horn blow outside, London ran over to look out of the front window. "Hey, that's Fatima! Let me go see what's up with her." London went out onto the porch and started to talk to Fatima.

Kenya took that opportunity to call Storm and check on him. He hadn't checked in with her since she had left Dallas. On the first ring, his phone went straight to voicemail. *Maybe it doesn't pick up in Mexico?* She decided then to call O.T. and see if he had heard from either Storm or Deacon. O.T. answered the phone on the fifth or sixth ring.

"Hello, hey, O.T. Have you spoke to the fellas yet?" Kenya was sounding cheerful.

"Naw, girl. And what fucking time is it anyhow? And why you calling me all early and shit?" O.T., who had been up at the club all night refused to return the politeness and wasn't in the mood to be questioned about the next nigga.

Kenya had forgotten all about the time difference. "Dang, bro, I'm sorry. My bad. Call me when you get up and tell Paris hello." She hung the phone up and peeked out the window. Kenya watched her sister and Fatima talk shit about a march that they were going to participate in, and smiled. She was proud of her twin and the woman she'd become despite all the obstacles that were thrown in her way.

While Kenya was watching the two of them, she had no idea that she wasn't the only one. Swift had been following Fatima around all morning since she had left the school and knew that eventually she'd lead him to his intended target: London Roberts. Smugly, he sat back in the car with her picture on the front seat.

Bingo! I knew that bitch would get with her girl sooner or later. Swift stared at London and Fatima as he licked his lips. The trained-to-kill assassin reached in the back seat and grabbed a magazine to pass time before preparing to earn his fee.

Finally, after twenty minutes of them talking, Fatima had to leave. She promised both girls a big surprise later when she returned. "Tell Kenya to be dressed and ready when I get back. The surprise is for both of y'all."

London assured Fatima that they would be ready and went in the house to take a nap. Swift sat in his car and waited for nightfall.

After about a half hour passed, another car pulled up in front of the house. The young guy driving the car got out and helped a little boy out of the rear seat. All of a sudden Kenya bolted out the door and grabbed the little boy up in her arms. It was her godson, Jaylin, and Young Foy. She tightly hugged them both.

"I'm so happy to see you guys. I think about y'all each and every day." Kenya kissed Jaylin on his jaws.

"I'm so proud of the job that you're doing with my godson. Raven would be proud too. You know she loved your crazy-acting ass!"

Young Foy blushed and reached into his car. "Here, this is for you. I'm about to do the damn thang!" He gave Kenya one of his new CDs that would be released soon. They talked for a short time before he had to leave. Young Foy and Jaylin said their good-byes to Kenya and were off.

As she waved to them on the edge of the curb, Swift took notice of her shape and beautiful facial features. He couldn't help but think how much better his intended target looked with makeup on than earlier. *Damn, too bad I have to kill the bitch. Maybe if I lie and promise to let her live she'll be nice and let me get the ass. I hate all that fighting and carrying on when a nigga trying to flat out take the pussy. It's one thing to kill a ho, but rape, hell naw! I ain't into that bullshit!*

Nevertheless, when nightfall finally came, she'd be dead just the same, with or without makeup even if she gave up the booty. Swift had a job to do—silence London Roberts for good.

Double Trouble on Dat Ass!

It had just gotten dark and the girls were getting ready to get dressed to go out to dinner with Fatima. She'd promised them a surprise and London could barely wait. She was the first to get in the shower and start to get herself together because she knew that Kenya would take practically all night getting dressed. While London was in the shower, Kenya took her cell phone off the charger and tried calling Storm again. Still, she got no answer. Once again it went straight to voicemail. Kenya looked at the clock before calling O.T. again and decided to call Alley Cats to see if he had spoken to his big brother yet. Something was wrong and she felt it. This wasn't like Storm not to call and check on her.

O.T. answered the phone after several rings. Between the loud noise of the club and him holding conversations with everyone else, he gave Kenya the response that she hated to hear. "Sorry, Kenya, nope, still no word. You know them dudes probably lying back on the beach, chillin' with some hoes! Naw, I'm just fucking with you." He tried to lighten the mood she was in. "Don't worry, girl, that sorry lovesick Negro you got is all right with his soft bitch-ass! They just probably somewhere teaching Royce how to dress!"

O.T. started to tease her and she felt much better. He even put his woman Paris on the phone, who also made her laugh. Paris let Kenya know that everything was running smooth at the club and she was keeping O.T. in order as well as Alley Cats. Kenya, still concerned, felt a little better when she hung up the phone, but her women's intuition wouldn't let her stop from worrying.

London got out of the shower and went into their room. "All right, girl, you next, and please don't take long to get ready. I don't want to be late. Fatima is always punctual."

Kenya got up and saluted London just like they were kids again. They both laughed.

While Kenya jumped in the shower, London started blow-drying her hair. With all the noise going on, they didn't hear Swift jimmy the lock on the back door and come inside the house. He was both quick and quiet.

That's where he had gotten his nickname from. Swift paused in the kitchen and listened carefully. Making sure the rest of the house was empty he crept into the living room. There he overheard noises coming from upstairs. Taking a deep breath, he ran his tongue over his teeth and headed in that direction. With the picture in his hand, Swift looked at it one last time, kissing it for good luck as he put it in his jacket. That was a habit that he started on his first murder-for-hire assignment and this was no different.

Swift reached in his inside pocket, removing a hit man's best friend. With expertise, he screwed the silencer on his pistol and slowly eased up the stairs. He took his time on each one. The age of the old house caused each one to make a creaking sound with every footstep. He finally made it to the top and was headed toward the direction of the sounds of the blow dryer. He was ready to do what he'd come to do, when all of a sudden the noise of the dryer stopped. *Damn!* Swift froze in his steps. Confused, he heard the bathroom door open and saw a shadow move out the side of his eye. Swift remained perfectly still as he gripped his gun tightly.

Kenya started talking. "See, sis, I told you that I wasn't gonna take all day. I was in and out!"

"I see. That's a first. What's the occasion?" London yelled back to her sister while checking to see what part of her hair was still damp.

Swift glanced around the dimly lit hallway as he thought, *Fuck it, two bitches for the price of one.* He'd been parked out front all day and he never saw her friend come in. He thought for sure that London was home alone. *I must be slipping, but oh well!* Swift questioned himself. Just then Swift heard one of the girls ask the other if she could come and help her with her hair. In a matter of seconds both girls were standing in the hallway and looking Swift dead in his face. *Well I'll be damned!* He had his gun raised and pointed at the sisters. Both of them, stunned, screamed loudly, not knowing what else to do.

"What the fuck?" Swift looked back and forth over and over and was confused. "Damn, it's two of you bitches!" He started to laugh and let his guard down. "Ain't this some bizarre shit!"

That's when the twins attacked him at the same time. It was another one of those situations where twins were famous for sharing the same thoughts. It took no words being passed for them both to react as one. Swift was trying his best to hold his own, but the girls had a lot of their father's blood in them. They were like wildcats. London and Kenya were definitely getting the best of Swift. He was feeling the wrath of the pain suffered, of the twins missing their parents and Gran. London also had Professor Kincade on her mind, while Kenya thought of Raven's murder. The girls' anger fueled their intense rage and it was on; fists being thrown, faces being socked and scratched, balls getting kicked, and eyes being gouged. The sisters had overcome a lot of things in their young lives and they were hell-bent determined to survive this as well.

Swift's gun had fallen on the floor and was kicked across the hallway into the darkness. All three were yelling and screaming as they struggled. The fight seemed to go on forever, when all of a sudden Swift's body jerked backward and went limp. He was motionless. The twins turned around and saw a huge figure in the corner with Swift's pistol in his hand. Kenya and London eyes grew wide as they awaited their fate. They then heard footsteps running up the stairs.

"Are you two all right? We knocked at the door and you didn't answer so we walked around the back and saw that the door was open. We heard yelling and rushed in.

Are you two hurt? What happened?" Thank God it was Fatima. She was crying and so were the twins. She was overjoyed that her friends were both safe. "I guess you two couldn't wait until dinner to get your big surprise could you?" Fatima wiped her eyes and smiled.

It was then that out of the shadows the man who had saved their lives appeared. London looked puzzled as she tried to focus on the massive-sized man. Kenya, relived, jumped to her feet. She ran over and embraced their savior.

"Oh my God, Brother Rasul, where did you come from? How did you get here? Never mind the questions. I'm so glad to see you! He was gonna kill us!"

Brother Rasul held her close and told her, "Remember I told you that I'd always have your back? Well, now you know it to be true." Kenya, out of breath from the struggle, had tears of joy streaming down her face. "I keep my word, no matter what!"

Fatima went to help London to her feet and introduced her to her big secret, Brother Rasul. He hugged London and told her that he was finally glad to meet her. Kenya and London were both dumbfounded and in shock at the fact that he was hooked up with their friend. The questions quickly began. Fatima explained to the twins that she met him in the hospital the day that their uncle was shot. She saw some of his family reading the Qur'an to him and joined in prayer with them. After that she and he became closer and closer.

Brother Rasul came and stood in the middle of the girls. "Excuse me, ladies, I hate to break this up, but we do have a dead man lying here I need to deal with."

The girls looked over to the other side of the hallway and hugged one another. The sight of Swift's curled-up, broken-neck deceased body caused them to have chills and turn away in utter disgust. Joining Brother Rasul, all the females went downstairs and sat down on the floor to regain their composure.

"We should call the police!" London yelled, not knowing what else to say. "We need to get that thug out of Gran's house!"

"Naw, London. We can't do that," Kenya chimed in. "We need to stop and think first."

"Yeah, that's right!" Fatima agreed. "We don't wanna get Rasul in any more trouble. He's already on probation from the shootout at Heads Up!"

"Not to worry!" Brother Rasul spoke again. "Calm down and let me use the phone. I got this!"

Now What?

The girls were all sitting close to each other as Brother Rasul's friends removed Swift's body through the back door. They had wrapped him in some old sheets that were in the basement and put him in the trunk of a car. As they pulled off, Brother Rasul approached the girls and showed them what he had found in the dead man's jacket. It was a picture of London. It apparently was taken at a PAID meeting. All three of the girls sat there with their mouths wide open not knowing what to think or say. They thought that the man was just a regular burglar who had broken in.

"That man was a professional hit man. Someone hired him to kill you, London!" Brother Rasul was trying his best to keep the girls calm, but at the same time he had to keep it real. This was serious, a serious matter. It wasn't over and he knew it. Just because Swift hadn't succeeded meant nothing. Whoever had paid him could probably easily afford to pay others. "Listen, little sister, I'll do all I can to find out who could have sent him, but in the meantime you need to lay low. That means no more meetings or school for the time being."

Kenya and Fatima both agreed with Brother Rasul. They trusted him with their lives; they had no other choice. Kenya wrapped her arms around London. "Why don't you fly back out to Dallas with me? It's no way in hell that they would look for you out there! You can stay with me and Storm in our guest room." Kenya had no idea that she was leading her sister straight into the belly of the beast.

After a lot of tears being shed, a distraught London lastly gave in and decided they were all correct. It would be in her best interest to take a break from school and go out west with Kenya. She needed a break anyway from all the limelight of PAID. Fatima promised to pack and send London's things to her as soon as she got back on campus and temporarily sign her out of all her classes.

Fatima and Brother Rasul drove both of the girls to the airport so they could catch a late flight. They said their farewells at the gate and sadly boarded the Texas-bound aircraft.

"Don't worry, London. You'll be safe when we get to Dallas. Storm and his boy Deacon have got that town on lock! We gonna be good!"

Kenya was trying endlessly to ease her sister's troubled mind, while she herself was a hot nervous wreck. When they landed and got their luggage, Kenya tried calling Storm's cell phone but unfortunately once again it went straight to voicemail. Needless to say she was starting to get beyond worried.

"Damn, why isn't his ass answering? He'd better not be fucking around with one of those island bitches!" Kenya slyly mumbled under her breath.

"Is everything all right?" London asked her sister as she looked directly in Kenya's face. She could tell that it was a problem. Even Ray Charles could.

"Yeah, I was just trying to call Storm. He must not be back in town yet, but it ain't a big deal. I'm straight!"

Kenya didn't know how she was going to break the news to him about London. After all, she had been lying. Well, sort of. He always thought her uncle was the only family she had, but bottom line it was time for her to face the music. Storm didn't have a choice in the matter. He would have to accept London and she in return would have to accept Storm and his crooked lifestyle.

Kenya tried not to worry as the pair took a taxi to her and Storm's condo. When they drove up, Kenya noticed all the lights on inside the house. She then made a mental note to curse Storm out for leaving all the lights on. He was, after all, the main one complaining about the bills.

"Well, this is it! I can't wait for you to see how I decorated it!" Kenya excitedly leaped out the cab, stretching her arms.

"So this is it, huh?" London looked around the quiet street that her sister had been calling home.

The driver set the bags on the curb, waited for his tip, and pulled off into the darkness of the night. Kenya and London picked them up slowly and made their way up to the door.

"Wait 'til you see it, London. It is nice as hell. It's everything I've ever dreamed about." Kenya stuck her key in the door, strangely discovering it was unlocked. *He must have really been in a rush.* Confused as to why Storm had carelessly left without securing their home Kenya pushed the door wide opened and stepped inside the entranceway. *What the fuck!* She couldn't believe her eyes and what she and her sister were faced with. "Oh my God! Oh my God! Oh nooooo!"

Kenya almost collapsed to the floor as London held her chest in utter disbelief. The karma that Kenya had put out in the universe had just come back to bite her dead in the ass!

The End 4 Now!